COLLATERAL DAMAGE

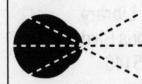

A STONE BARRINGTON NOVEL

COLLATERAL DAMAGE

STUART WOODS

THORNDIKE PRESS
A part of Gale, Cengage Learning

Detroit • New York • San Francisco • New Haven, Conn • Waterville, Maine • London

GALE
CENGAGE Learning®

LIBRARY OF CONGRESS CATALOGING-IN-PUBLICATION DATA

Woods, Stuart.
    Collateral damage : a Stone Barrington novel / by Stuart Woods.
      pages ; cm. — (Thorndike Press large print basic)
    ISBN-13: 978-1-4104-5492-8 (hardcover)
    ISBN-10: 1-4104-5492-4 (hardcover)
    1. Barrington, Stone (Fictitious character)—Fiction. 2. Private
investigators—New York (State)—New York—Fiction. 3. New York
(N.Y.)—Fiction. 4. Large type books. I. Title.
    PS3573.O642C67 2013
    813'.54—dc23   2012043588

Published in 2013 by arrangement with G.P. Putnam's Sons, a member of Penguin Group (USA) Inc.

Printed in the United States of America
1 2 3 4 5 6 7 17 16 15 14 13

COLLATERAL DAMAGE

1

Elaine's, late.

Stone Barrington opened the taxi door. "Wait for me," he said. "I won't be long." He got out of the cab and looked around. The yellow awning was gone, but "Elaine's" was still painted on the darkened windows. A film of soap obscured the interior, but Stone found a bare spot and put his hands up to shield from the glare. What he saw was, in short, nothing.

The book jackets, photographs, and posters that had adorned the walls for forty-seven years were gone. The bar and mirrors behind it were still there, but there were no stools. The dining room contained no tables or chairs and no blue-checkered tablecloths. The two old pay phones still hung on the wall near the cashier's stand at the bar; they had always been the only phones in the place.

For a tiny moment Stone could hear the

babble of a crowded room, chairs scraping, people calling the length of the room to say hello to a friend. Then a passing bus obliterated the sounds and returned Stone to the present. He got back into the cab and gave the driver his home address.

His cell phone buzzed at his belt. "Hello?"

"It's Dino. Where are you?"

"At Elaine's."

A brief silence, then: "You shouldn't do that."

"You're right," Stone said. "The memory is better than the reality. Have you had dinner?"

"I was just thinking about it."

"Where's Viv?"

"She's working."

"Come over and I'll make you some pasta."

"You, yourself?"

"Me, myself. I can cook, you know."

"There was a rumor, but I never believed it."

"Fifteen minutes."

"Okay. Oh, how are we dressing?"

"Unarmed," Stone said.

"I'm always armed."

"Then you can check your gun at the door."

"Whatever you say."

"How late is Viv working?"

"Until ten."

"Tell her to come over after, and I'll save her something."

"I'll see if she's brave enough."

"See ya." Stone hung up.

At home, he shucked off his jacket in the kitchen and checked the fridge. It was stuffed, as usual. Helene was an overshopper, and she liked to be ready for anything.

Stone found some Italian sausages, some mushrooms, some broccoli rabe, and some garlic. He sliced the sausages and tossed them into a skillet with a little olive oil, and they began to sizzle. He ran some water into a pot and put it on to boil for the pasta. He found some ziti in a cupboard and tossed it into the boiling water, then he chopped some onion and the garlic and tossed them into the pan with the sausages, followed by the mushrooms and rabe.

Dino came into the kitchen and tossed his coat on a chair. "Jesus, that smells pretty good," he admitted.

"Be ready in ten, fifteen minutes," Stone said. "Pour us a drink."

Dino went to the kitchen bar, filled a pair of glasses with ice, then filled one with his usual Johnnie Walker Black scotch and the

9

other with Stone's Knob Creek bourbon, then handed it to Stone. "Okay, what was the place like?"

"Bereft of all humankind and Elaine. Bereft of everything, come to that." The contents of the place had been sold at auction, along with Elaine's personal effects. Stone had bid on some books but didn't get them.

"You know," Dino said, taking a bite of his scotch, "I think she'd be happy that we can't find a new place."

"She wasn't that mean-spirited," Stone pointed out.

"She was about other joints. I'm still afraid to go to Elio's." Elio was a former Elaine's headwaiter who had opened his own restaurant a couple of blocks down Second Avenue.

"Yeah, me too. I only went once, just to say hello to Elio, but I never let her find out. She would have stabbed me with a fork."

"Or worse."

Stone found a hunk of Parmigianino-Reggiano in the fridge and dug the grater out of a drawer. He drained the pasta, forked some onto two plates, dumped some sausage onto the plates and grated a lot of the cheese over them, then he set them on the table and got a bottle of Amarone out of the wine closet and opened it. "Sit yourself down," he said.

Dino did, and they both ate hungrily.

When Viv showed up, they hadn't even cleared the table; they were just sitting there, drinking and talking.

"Just like Elaine's," Viv said. "Without Elaine."

2

Jasmine Shazaz sat in a car parked in Mount Street, London, with a cell phone in her hand. She watched as, fifty yards away, a government Jaguar pulled up in front of the Connaught Hotel and stopped. A man in a dark suit waved the uniformed doorman out of the way as he reached for the car's rear door, then opened it himself. Another man Jasmine recognized from newspapers and television as a high government official left the hotel and walked toward the open car door, got in and hipped his way across the seat to the left side.

The Special Branch detective, who had been holding the door open, got in behind him and closed the door. The car moved a few feet to Mount Street, the driver looked both ways, then turned left.

Jasmine pressed the phone button on her smartphone, chose a number, and looked out her windscreen. It would take three seconds to connect the call. She pressed the button. "Three, two, one," she counted, and as she spoke the word "zero," the glass front of the Porsche dealer's building at the bottom of Mount Street blew outward, followed by a large ball of flame.

The explosion rocked her car and enveloped the government Jaguar, which was directly in front of the Porsche dealer. The car took the full force of the explosion and was lifted off the pavement, rolling over. The gas tank exploded, creating a secondary ball of flame. The job was done.

Jasmine put her car in gear and, ignoring the broken glass and small rubble on the hood of her car, made a U-turn from her parking space, drove up to South Audley Street, crossed it, then a block later turned left into Park Lane. Sixty seconds later she was in Hyde Park, and five minutes after that she took a seat at the Serpentine Restaurant in the park and perused the menu. Her lunch date arrived a moment later and sat down.

"I believe there was some sort of explosion over around Berkeley Square," he said, in perfect, upper-class English, though his appearance was Mediterranean, perhaps even Middle Eastern.

"That must be why we're hearing all those

fire engines and police cars," she said.

"Let's see if there's any news," he said, taking a smartphone from his jacket pocket and switching it on. A moment later they were watching ITV News as a slide appeared. "Breaking News," it said.

A young woman, hastily arranging her skirt, gazed into the camera, then read from a sheet of paper in her hand. "ITV News has a reliable report that some sort of bomb has gone off in Mayfair, perhaps in Mount Street. Our reporter, Jason Banks, has just arrived at the scene. Jason?"

The camera jerked about, then stabilized. A man was clipping a microphone to his lapel, then he looked up and saw the camera. "Good afternoon, Jane," he said. "I'm standing a few yards from the northwest corner of Berkeley Square." He looked over his shoulder, and the camera zoomed in past him. "As you can see, there has been a very large explosion up there, and it appears that the location was the building housing the Porsche sports car dealership. The front of the building has disappeared, and the fire brigade has just arrived on the scene and are connecting their hose pipes as we speak. The events have only just occurred — I and my crew were on the other side of the square, interviewing a police spokesman about a robbery that occurred in Bruton Place a little over an hour ago. The policeman we were interviewing immediately called New Scotland Yard and reported the explosion, then ran toward the burning building. We moved our equipment as quickly as we could, and this is as close as we could get."

"Jason," the anchor said, holding a finger to an ear, "we're just getting a report from a Westminster correspondent that the foreign secretary is lunching at the Connaught Hotel, about fifty meters up the street from the blast location, and we have a unit on the way there to interview him and see if we can get any further information."

The camera went back to Jason Banks. He was moving up the street to get closer to the burning building. "Jane, we've been able to get a few yards closer, and if our camera can zoom in on that burning motorcar sitting on top of two other cars . . . Zoom in on it, damn you!" The camera zoomed in on the burning car. "That was, until a few moments ago, a Jaguar motorcar, and as you can see, the front number plate begins with the letters FO, identifying it as a government vehicle assigned to the Foreign Office. We can only hope that is a horrible coincidence and that the foreign

15

secretary is still enjoying his after-lunch port at the Connaught."

A police car with its lights and siren on came close to running down Jason Banks as it raced toward the burning vehicle. "Shit!" the reporter yelled. "That was close. Let me see if I can get a word." He began jogging toward the police car, which had stopped a few yards away and was disgorging two high-ranking police officers, judging from their insignia.

"Excuse me, Inspector," Banks said, thrusting a microphone at one of them, "but does that number plate on that Jaguar belong to the foreign secretary?"

The response to his shouted question was a stout forearm across the face, nearly causing him to eat his microphone. "Get out of the way, you bloody fool!" the officer yelled.

Banks fell back, nursing his lips with the back of his hand. "As you can see, Jane, the inspector is in no mood to chat. Perhaps you can get a confirmation on this number plate." He began reading the letters and numbers.

"Yes, Jason, we'll do that," the anchor said, scribbling down the numbers, then ripping a sheet off a pad and throwing it at someone off camera. "Run that number down!" she shouted at the person, then she recovered herself. "If you are just joining us, what we know so far is . . ."

The man switched off his smartphone. "I think we can order lunch now," he said to Jasmine, while beckoning a waiter.

"Order me the Dover sole," Jasmine said. "And I think, perhaps, a bottle of champagne would be in order."

3

Holly Barker, assistant director of Central Intelligence, took her seat at the table in the conference room of her boss, Katharine Rule Lee, the director of Central Intelligence. She was well rested after a couple of days off following a meeting between the presidents of the United States and Mexico, which she had attended in company with the director.

The final seats at the table were filled at fifteen seconds before nine o'clock, according to the GPS-controlled clock on the wall, and at the stroke of nine, the director entered the room and sat down.

"Good morning, ladies and gentlemen," Kate Lee said. "Thank you for coming. Holly, what's on our agenda for this morning?"

"Good morning, Director," Holly replied. "DDO Lance Cabot has three reports from foreign stations, to start us off." She nod-

18

ded at Lance.

Cabot shuffled some papers. "Our station in Lagos, Nigeria, was the target of a Molotov cocktail earlier today. The bottle shattered on the wrought-iron fence, and only slightly splashed the facade of the building. A Marine guard extinguished the flame almost immediately. No one has, as yet, claimed credit, but we suspect either an antigovernment insurgent group or, perhaps, the government itself. Take your pick." He set aside a sheet of paper, then continued. "We have penetrated the administrative offices of an army base in . . ." Lance stopped as a middle-aged woman walked behind him, tapped him on the shoulder, and placed a sheet of paper in front of him. He read it, then looked up.

"What is it, Lance?" Kate asked.

"Tom Riley, London station chief, is on the phone with something important."

Kate reached for the phone near her and pressed the line button and the speaker control. "Good morning, Tom. We are assembled at the regular morning briefing. Everyone is here. What's happening?"

A large flat-screen monitor flickered to life and revealed a man in his late forties with an iron-gray, old-fashioned crew cut. "Good morning, Director, everybody. Local TV news is running a breaking news report of a large explosion at a Porsche dealership just off Berkeley Square. One of our people was lunching at the Connaught and saw the foreign secretary leave the dining room perhaps three minutes earlier. A Jaguar that might well be his official car was passing the dealership when the explosion took place, and anyone inside the car is now dead. We're awaiting the running of the plate number, which begins with FO, indicating a Foreign Office vehicle." News footage of a burning car filled the screen.

"Tom," Kate said, "if the foreign secretary was in the car, do you have an opinion as to whether this was intended as an attack on him or if he was just at the wrong place at the wrong time?"

"I'm afraid that would be much too large a coincidence to be credible," Riley said. "Hang on, I've just had confirmation that the number plate belonged to the foreign secretary's car, and our own man reports seeing the man get into the car in front of the Connaught."

"Any thoughts on the perpetrators?" Kate asked.

"Too many possibilities to make an educated guess at this point, but we're on it, and we have good sources at New Scotland

Yard, so we should have an idea soon."

"Anything else, Tom?"

"Not at this time, Director."

"Keep us posted, then." She pressed the button, and the screen went dark. "Not every day we have the assassination of a cabinet member in a major European ally," she said to the table at large. "Lance? Anything?"

"Nothing that would have led us to anticipate such an event, Director," Cabot replied. "Not a peep. I find it interesting that the perpetrators decided to take out a building and God knows who and what else at a corner of London's most famous square, in an effort to take out one man. I think there's a statement there."

"Director," Holly said, "given the timing, there must have been an operative on or near the site to set off the explosion."

"Good point, Holly," Kate said. "Will you call Tom back when we're done and ask him to get every possible angle of surveillance footage from New Scotland Yard? London has thousands of these cameras. I'm sure Special Branch is already reviewing the recording, but we might be able to spot somebody not in their files."

"Yes, Director," Holly said, making a note. As she did, Holly had a thought, but it was

21

too soon to bring it up, and certainly not in this meeting.

"Did I detect something just now, Holly? An idea?"

"Just a wild guess, Director. I'd like to run it down a little before I make an ass of myself."

That gained a chuckle from the dozen men and women present.

"Oh, go on, Holly, I'd like a view into your frontal lobe. Entertain us."

Holly shrugged. "If you insist, Director. You will recall that, last week, a London asset of ours and his brother were involved in planting bombs at an L.A. location. They are both dead now."

"For which we can thank the appropriate person at this table," Kate said.

Lance lifted an eyebrow. "Did those two gentlemen have an accomplice we are unaware of, Holly?"

"They had a sister," Holly said, and the room became very still.

"Ah, yes," Lance said. "Remind us."

"Jasmine," Holly said, "the youngest of the three Shazaz siblings."

"Whereabouts?" Kate asked, looking at Lance.

Lance merely shook his head.

"Holly? A guess?"

"Her two brothers lived in London," Kate said. "Perhaps she did, too."

"They had a rather elegant house, as I recall. Where was it?"

"Cheyne Walk, beside the Thames, in Chelsea."

"Ah, yes. When you speak to Tom, raise that subject, please. I'd like to know where Ms. Shazaz is, or when she was last sighted."

"She was in Palo Alto when the West Coast bombs were made," Holly said. She did not mention that one of the bombs had been a nuclear device, because she didn't know how many of the people in the room knew that. Lance probably did, but maybe not the others.

"Oh," the director said. It was a very expressive word. "Why the hell didn't we bag her?"

Lance spoke up. "We didn't bag anybody until after the Palo Alto operation had been shut down," he said, "and intel led us to believe that she was already out of the country when we bagged her brothers."

"Did intel indicate where out of the country?" Kate asked.

"No, Director, not at the time. Perhaps we have a better idea now."

"Could this be a revenge killing?" Kate asked. "Or is there a larger motive afoot?"

23

Holly spoke. "It might be said that the foreign secretary was connected to recent events in California, in the person of the head of MI-6, who was present in L.A."

"Perhaps you'd better give that lady a jingle," Kate said, "and let her know of your, ah . . . opinion. I would hate to hear of some later event that we might have helped to stop."

"With your permission, I'll make that call now," Holly said.

"Please do so."

Holly rose and returned to her office next to the director's, her heart beating a little faster.

4

Holly dialed the London direct line for Felicity Devonshire, known as "Architect," head of MI-6.

"Yes?" a male voice asked.

"This is Holly Barker, assistant director of intelligence, calling from Langley, Virginia, for Architect."

"Architect is presently unavailable," the man said. "I'll say you called." He hung up without further ado.

Well, that was short, Holly thought. She might as well go back to the meeting. Then her phone rang. "Holly Barker."

"It's Felicity. I'm sorry my assistant was short with you. As you can imagine, we're in the middle of a flap here."

"The director asked me to call and give you an idea that arose at our daily briefing this morning."

"I'd be grateful for any suggestion, of course."

"It occurred to us that this act might be revenge for the deaths of Ari Shazaz, aka Hamish McCallister, and his brother, Mohammad."

Felicity was briefly silent. "Well, that's a stretch, but . . ."

"Are you aware that the Shazazes have a sister who was complicit in the bomb making?"

"One moment." Felicity covered the phone and could be heard to speak authoritatively to someone in the room. "No, we are not aware of that. Do you have details?"

"Her name is Jasmine, she is the youngest of the three siblings, and she may have shared Hamish's London residence, in Cheyne Walk. I'm afraid that's all we have, but we would certainly be grateful for anything you learn."

"Of course," Felicity said, "and I thank you for the call, Holly. Please give my very best to Kate and thank her for thinking of us. Now, if you'll excuse me . . ."

"Of course." But Felicity had already hung up. Holly was about to return to the briefing when her phone rang again. "Holly Barker."

"Holly, this is Tim Coleman. Is the director available?" Coleman was the president's chief of staff.

"Good morning, Tim. She's in the daily intelligence briefing at the moment, but if it's urgent I can interrupt."

"No, don't do that. You're in the loop on this, so I'll tell you, and you can tell her."

"All right."

"The Oak Ridge nuclear plant has run some tests on the fissionable material found in the California device. It's a match for a smaller sample that turned up a few months ago that is suspected to have originated in Iran."

The hairs on Holly's arm stood up. "That hasn't been confirmed?"

"No, but we have samples of the enriched uranium from the stores of all the other nuclear-capable countries, and it doesn't match any of them, so it has to be from either Iran or North Korea."

"I see," Holly said. "Is anything else known about the California material?"

"No, but the fact that the late Dr. Kharl supplied the material is another connection to one of those two countries."

Dr. Kharl, who had assembled the California device, was recently deceased, an order that Holly had transmitted from the director, after presidential approval. He had been instrumental in the Pakistani nuclear weapons program, as well as the North Korean program, and had been thought to be available to just about anyone with the cash.

"I agree," Holly said. "Anything else, before I drop this bombshell on the director?"

"Just don't expand the loop. See you later." Coleman hung up.

Holly hung up, too. That meant she couldn't bring it up at the briefing. She went back into the room and waited, trying to hide her impatience, while Lance concluded his report. He was talking of the penetration of an Iranian army unit connected with that country's nuclear program.

The director glanced at her. "Ladies and gentlemen," she said when Lance had finished, "unless there's something else of level one importance, you'll have to hold any other information until tomorrow's briefing. Thank you all." She stood up, signaling that everyone should leave, and with a motion of her head indicated that Holly should follow her.

Holly left the room and followed the director to her office, where she took the indicated seat.

"You've learned something new," Kate said.

"First, Felicity and her people were not aware of the existence of Jasmine Shazaz, but now they are, and they will be checking out the Cheyne Walk house. I told her about that on my own authority, reasoning that MI-6 could get in there faster and more thoroughly than London station could, and with less of a local flap, and I think she'll feel obligated to share."

"I concur."

"A second thing: Tim Coleman called and asked for you, but declined to interrupt your briefing. Since I'm in the loop he told me that Oak Ridge has determined that the enriched uranium in the California device most likely came from either Iran or North Korea, since it was introduced by Dr. Kharl and is not a match for that of any of the programs we're familiar with."

"I'm glad you didn't blurt that out in the briefing," Kate said.

"No, ma'am, I know the loop is small. I don't even know if it includes Lance."

"You and I are the loop in this agency," Kate replied, "and we're going to keep it that way. Outside, it's the Secret Service, Mike Freeman of Strategic Services, and Stone Barrington, who somehow managed to stop the clock on that thing without blowing us all to kingdom come, and Dino Bacchetti. And the president, of course, which accounts for Tim Coleman being inside, too."

"There's one other," Holly said.

"And who might that be?" Kate asked sharply.

"The reporter from *Vanity Fair,* Kelli Keane, who was in the room with the device when it was stopped."

"Good God," Kate moaned.

"Stone had a very serious word with her afterward, and impressed on her the importance of the event never having taken place."

"Do you think that will be enough to keep her lid on? I mean, she's a journalist, for God's sake!"

"Stone thought she got the message."

"Did he threaten her?"

"I don't believe so."

"Holly, I want you to leave for New York immediately, by the fastest conveyance available, pick her up, sit her down in a quiet room, and frighten her to the bottom of her soul."

Holly stood up. "Yes, ma'am. Is there anything else?"

"Do you have any doubts about the ability of Stone Barrington to keep this to himself forever? And Dino Bacchetti? It was his gun."

"No, ma'am, I have no doubts about either of them. They're both under contract to the Agency as consultants and, as such, have the highest security clearance."

"Good. Get going."

Holly went to her office, picked up a phone and called the director of transportation. "This is Assistant Director Holly Barker. Is there a chopper on the pad right now?"

"Yes, ma'am," the man replied, "but it's leaving momentarily for Dulles, to pick up a visiting dignitary."

"Cancel that flight immediately and find another way to transport the dignitary. I want the aircraft fueled and the flight plan filed for New York by the time I can get down there." She hung up without another word, got her ready bag from her closet, and headed for the elevator.

5

The rotors were already turning on the brand-new Sikorsky X2 helicopter, not even certified yet, but on loan to the Agency. Holly hadn't expected this, but she was looking forward to the ride. She hopped into the cabin and buckled in.

After what seemed like only a moment, the sleek machine was flying north, directly into the D.C. no-fly zone and at no more than a thousand feet. She put on her headset. "Hey," she said to the pilot, "aren't we a little low?"

"On purpose, ma'am," the pilot said. "No traffic over Washington at this altitude."

"Can this thing really break two hundred fifty knots?"

"That's classified, ma'am, but you have an honest face, so yes, ma'am. It's the fastest chopper ever, and it's all mine! I guess you got your seat belt fastened?"

"I have."

"Well, right after we blow past the White House, I'm going to show you some climb performance."

"You go right ahead." Holly looked out her window and the White House blew by, indeed; she could see the ground-to-air missile launchers on the roof. Suddenly, the helicopter raised its nose, and Holly looked over the pilot's shoulder at the speed tape on the glass cockpit's pilot's flight display. It was moving too fast for her to keep up with. Then they leveled at twelve thousand feet, leaving her stomach in the air, and the climb seemed to have taken but a moment.

"You enjoy that?" the pilot asked.

"I've always loved roller coasters," she replied.

"We'll be on the East Side pad in less than an hour."

"Does the satphone work?" she asked.

"On this bird, *everything* works, ma'am."

Holly picked up the phone, called the Agency's East Side facility and asked for the agent in charge.

He came on the line immediately. "Holly Barker?"

"That's right. I'm inbound for the East Side Heliport, ETA forty-five minutes. I need a vehicle to meet me, and I need an immediate location for a Kelli Keane, a

33

writer for *Vanity Fair* magazine. She's freelance and may work from home."

"We're on it."

"Send a team to find her, stat, then politely but firmly bring her to your location. Clear a room for me to have a quiet chat with her. No video or audio, is that clear?"

"Clear."

"Over and out." Holly hung up the phone and sat back to watch the countryside stream past her window.

Kelli Keane was having lunch with a woman friend at a chic downtown restaurant when her cell phone went off. "Kelli Keane."

"Ms. Keane, my name is Carlson, and I am a federal agent. I need to speak to you alone at the front door of the restaurant immediately. My people will settle your check, so go there now, understood?"

"No, not understood."

"If it will be more convenient for you, I can send two agents into the restaurant to assist you outside. Would you prefer that?"

"All right, all right, how long?"

"Ten seconds." The line went dead.

"Carolyn," Kelli said to her companion, "it seems something urgent has come up and I'll have to leave, maybe for a few minutes, maybe longer. The check will be taken care of." Kelli looked toward the front door and saw two large men in dark suits walk in and look around. "Gotta go," she said to the astonished Carolyn. The door was open when she got there.

"Straight ahead," one of the men said, assisting her along by the elbow and nearly lifting her off her feet. She found herself in the rear seat of a black SUV between the two men, and the windows were blacked out.

"All right," Kelli said, "what the hell is going on here?"

"Be quiet," the man said. "Someone wishes to speak with you. We'll reach your first destination in twenty minutes."

"Then what?" she asked, but no one answered her.

Twenty minutes later, the car drove into an underground garage and stopped at an elevator. Several floors later, she was put into what appeared to be a small living room, furnished with a sofa, chairs, and a small dining table. The door closed behind her before she could ask where they were.

After the helicopter landed, Holly held the headset mike to her lips. "That was just amazing," she said to the pilot. "Thanks so much." Then she hopped out of the chopper and, eight steps later, into a black SUV. Six minutes after that, the car went underground, and she was rising in the elevator. The AIC was waiting for her.

"She's in a holding room," he said.

"Remember, no video, no audio, and no peeking. Got it?"

"Got it." He led the way down the hall, opened the door, and closed it behind her.

Holly found Kelli Keane sitting at the table, trying to use her iPhone. She recognized her from having seen her at The Arrington hotel in Los Angeles, but they had not met. "Your phone won't work," she said.

Kelli put the phone back into her purse. "You look familiar," she said. "Were you in L.A. a couple of weeks ago?"

Holly sat down. "While you were there, some unusual events occurred, and Stone Barrington had a conversation with you about them. Remember?"

"Of course I remember."

"Then stop remembering," Holly said. She took a pad from her jacket pocket and uncapped her pen. "I want the names of everyone to whom you have spoken about those events."

Kelli looked her in the eye. "Stone asked me not to speak of that, and I have not spoken of it."

36

"How about your boyfriend, James Rutledge? What did you tell him?"

"I told him I had a grand time at The Arrington, nothing else."

"What about Graydon Carter at *Vanity Fair*?"

"I don't work directly with him, but I haven't spoken with my editor about it, either. I just turned in my piece, which mentioned nothing about it."

"Who else have you not told about those events?" Holly asked.

"The entire world," Kelli said. "They are all among the people I have not told about that experience. One of the men who brought me here said that this was my first destination. What did he mean by that? Where is my next destination?"

"You have two choices," Holly said. "One is wherever you wish in Manhattan. The other is the Guantanamo naval base, on the island of Cuba, for an indeterminate time."

"I'll take Manhattan," Kelli replied, "never mind the Bronx and Staten Island, too."

Holly allowed herself a small smile. "I appear to have made my point."

"You certainly have," Kelli said.

"One other thing," Holly replied.

"What's that?"

"For the remainder of your life on this

planet, you will not experience a remembrance of those events."

"What events?" Kelli asked.

Holly got up, rapped on the door, and it was opened from the outside. "Take the elevator to the basement," she said to Kelli. "A car is waiting for you."

"And my destination?"

"Anywhere in Manhattan. Back to the restaurant, if you like."

Kelli consulted her watch. "My friend will either be gone by now or very drunk. Home will do."

"Home it is. Thank you for your co-operation, Ms. Keane."

"Don't mention it."

"You neither," Holly said, pressing the elevator button.

6

Holly used an empty office and called Kate Lee on a secure line.

"How was the helicopter ride?" Kate asked.

"Spectacular."

"And your mission?"

"Accomplished. The lady has suffered a complete and permanent memory loss regarding those events. I believe she fully appreciates that necessity."

"Keep an eye on her anyway," Kate said. "I'm sending the chopper back for you tomorrow morning for a ten A.M. departure, sharp. I'd like you to bring Stone Barrington, Dino Bacchetti, and Mike Freeman with you."

"I'll get right on that," she said, thinking of Stone.

"There'll be a quick lunch and a briefing at the White House. The chopper will take you directly there."

"Yes, ma'am," Holly said.

"Confirm ASAP that the others will arrive with you. Goodbye." The director hung up.

Holly dialed Stone's office and got Joan, his secretary.

"Hey, Holly," Joan said, "always glad to hear from you."

"Thanks, Joan. Is he available?"

"Certainly."

He picked up. "Stone Barrington."

"It's Holly. How are you?"

"As well as can be expected," Stone said.

Holly laughed. "If you can scrape up the energy, I have two invitations for you."

"I'll manage."

"The first: you're invited to take me to dinner tonight, then do terrible things to me in bed."

"I can handle that."

"The second: please call Dino and Mike Freeman and ask them to be at the East Side Heliport tomorrow morning for a ten A.M. departure for Washington. There will be lunch at the White House, followed by a briefing."

"What sort of briefing?"

"Don't ask."

"Oh, *that* kind of briefing."

"Right. And don't tell, either. Make sure that Dino and Mike know that. Top secret.

They'll be back for dinner."

"You intrigue me."

"Of course I do, silly, why else would you want to do terrible things to me in bed?"

"When are you coming?"

"I'm already in town, but I have some calls to make. I'll be at your place around seven."

"Use your key. I'll be upstairs."

Stone called Dino and Mike; the mention of the White House got their attention and their consent to travel and their promise to shut up about it.

Holly let herself into Stone's house a little after seven and took the elevator up to the master suite. "Hello? Anybody there?"

"I'm in the shower," Stone yelled back. "Join me or make yourself at home."

Holly stripped off her clothes, threw them on a chair, and joined him. Big hug, big kiss.

"What brings you to town?" Stone asked, scrubbing her back with a soft brush.

"You do. You and Kelli Keane."

"Are you sleeping with her, too?"

"Nope, just you. She and I had a chat."

"Uh-oh."

"Exactly."

"I had that chat with her in L.A."

"The director was anxious that your suggestions to her be underlined in a memorable way."

"Did you slap her around?"

"It didn't come to that — she got the message."

"But you would have slapped her around, if she had been slow to catch on?"

"I don't slap people around, I have people who handle that sort of thing." She was scrubbing his back, now, then his front. "I see that I have excited your interest," she said, stroking him to fullness.

"You are very perceptive."

"Are we clean enough now?"

"I believe we are."

Holly turned off the water, stepped out of the shower and toweled herself, then she grabbed a dry bath sheet and worked on Stone.

"This is the most fun I've had for some time," Stone said.

"Stick around," she said, "it's going to get better." And she was right.

When they had exhausted themselves, then showered off the sweat, Holly sat on the bed, toweling her hair. "Where are we dining?"

"The Four Seasons all right?"

"That seedy old joint? I wish we could go to Elaine's."

"So do I, but in the circumstances, the Four Seasons will have to do."

They dined for two hours at one of the world's most elegant restaurants, then returned to Stone's house for a repeat performance of their earlier assignation.

"Holly," Stone said when they had finished, "is something bad going to happen?"

"I and my people work hard every day to see that nothing bad happens, and we're good at it."

"I feel so much better," Stone said, snuggling up to her and falling asleep.

7

The group convened at the East Side Heliport in time to see the sleek new helicopter set down.

"Wow," Stone said, "what is that?"

"I know what it is," Mike Freeman said. "We've already ordered one." Mike was the CEO of Strategic Services, the largest private security firm in the world, and he often knew about things like this before others did.

"Why am I not surprised?" Stone asked.

Holly directed Stone to the left cockpit seat, while she sat in the rear with Dino and Mike.

Stone looked at the instrument panel and controls. "Don't worry, I'm not going to ask you how all this stuff works," he said to the pilot.

"Thanks," the pilot replied, running through a checklist. "Ever flown a helicopter?"

"Once," Stone said. "I'd rather not think about it."

The engines revved, and the chopper leaped off the pad and turned down the East River, gaining altitude quickly. Next thing Stone knew they were over Cape May and turning for Washington.

The pilot was constantly on the radio, and Stone could hear the conversations on his headset. It was obvious that this was no ordinary flight; they were getting special treatment from Air Traffic Control.

"How do I get them to talk to me like that when I'm flying my Citation Mustang?" Stone asked.

"Easy — just have the White House file your flight plan."

They had descended rapidly over the city, and Stone saw the White House directly ahead. A crowd was gathered under the West Wing portico, and someone was speaking into a small forest of microphones.

"That press conference is for your benefit," the pilot said. "Keeps the press around that side while I'm unloading you on the presidential pad."

Then the helicopter was on the ground, and they were hurrying toward a door held open by a Secret Service agent. Shortly, they were in the Oval Office, where menus from

45

the White House Mess were distributed. Everybody ordered sandwiches, and as they were delivered, the president walked into the room and sat down in a comfortable chair.

"Good morning, Holly, Stone, Dino, and Mike, and thank you all for coming."

Everybody voiced greetings, then they were handed trays, and the president's mouth seemed always too full for him to speak. The trays were taken away, and he stood up. "Come on, we're going to have coffee downstairs."

Stone thought that meant the White House Mess, but when they got on the elevator it went down quickly for a greater distance than he had anticipated.

They stepped off the elevator and into a vestibule, where a naval officer distributed picture IDs that were hung around their necks, then they were ushered into a large conference room with many screens on the walls.

Stone immediately recognized Steve Rifkin, who had been in charge of the presidential Secret Service detail at The Arrington; Tim Coleman, the White House chief of staff; and another two men whom he knew to be bomb specialists, along with a man Stone recognized from newspaper photographs as the head of the Secret Service. Kate Lee was already seated at the conference table, at the opposite end from her husband, the president. She was the first to speak.

"Good morning, Mr. President, ladies and gentlemen. You will have noticed that the group around this table — the president, the chief of staff, the chief of the Secret Service, and I excepted — were in the suite at The Arrington when a nuclear device was discovered in a trunk. The people responsible for building and delivering it are now deceased, so those of you in this room are the only persons with direct knowledge of that day's events. You've been asked here for what we hope will be the final briefing on this subject, so that all of you will understand what could have occurred at The Arrington if you had been less vigilant, and the vital importance of keeping every detail of those events confined to the people around this table. No other person in the government not in this room has the knowledge that you are about to possess. I'll turn you over to Steve Rifkin now."

"Thank you, Director," Rifkin said. "Since you were all present at the scene you know what occurred. Our purpose today is to fill in the blanks that some of you may not know. Our chief bomb technician here has put together a short film, cobbled together from photographs, film and sat shots, along with computer-generated animation, that will give you an accurate idea of what might have happened that day. He was the only person to work on the film, and he is the narrator. What you will see is the only existing version of the film. All the other materials have been destroyed, and after you see it, it will be sealed, placed in a vault at the new Will Lee Presidential Library, which is about to begin construction in Delano, Georgia, and not made public until fifty years after the death of President Lee — and then, only with the consent of whoever is president at that time."

The lights went down and the film began, displayed on four screens in the situation room, so that no one would have to crane his neck to view it.

The first image was the planet from outer space; the shot zoomed in to contain California, then farther, to embrace Los Angeles. The zoom slowed as the grounds and buildings of The Arrington came into view.

"This was to be the origin of the worst attack of any kind on the United States in the country's history," the bomb chief's voice said, as the view zoomed in farther to the

48

building containing the suite, then traveled into the bedroom, where a closet door opened to reveal a Louis Vuitton steamer trunk.

"This is the suite occupied by this man" — a photograph appeared on-screen — "born Ari Shazaz, but known to others as Hamish McCallister, who was born of a Scottish mother and an Algerian father, then raised in Britain and educated at Eton and Oxford. We now know that his father, who was divorced from his mother and remarried, fathered another son and a daughter, and was a close associate of Osama bin Laden from a time when they were both students together in Saudi Arabia. Mr. Shazaz was caught up in a sweep of al Qaeda operatives by CIA and MI-6 personnel in a house in Cairo and was almost immediately transported to the naval base at Guantánamo, Cuba. He was held there for nearly three years, during which time he never disclosed his identity, in spite of enhanced interrogation. He died there of a stroke, after having been waterboarded more than fifty times. His sons and daughter, all of whom had had intensive Islamic education, became radicalized by his capture and death.

"Al Qaeda operatives made contact with

them, and a cell was formed, funded by Osama bin Laden personally. After bin Laden's death in a Navy SEAL raid last year, they dedicated themselves to perpetrating a monumental terrorist attack on the United States in revenge for the deaths of their father and bin Laden. They enlisted this man" — another photograph appeared — "Dr. Ahmed Kharl, who had been a highly placed scientist in the Pakistani nuclear program and who later worked on both the Iranian and North Korean programs. When the Pakistani program was shut down, he became a freelancer. He designed a device that would fit into a large trunk and had various parts machined at diverse shops, so that no one person ever knew what was being constructed. The parts were smuggled into the United States, along with three kilograms of enriched uranium, and Dr. Kharl traveled to Palo Alto, California, where he met with the three Shazaz siblings and assembled the device in an apartment rented by them.

"The device and three smaller, non-nuclear bombs were transported to Los Angeles from the San Jose airport to a hangar at Santa Monica Airport. The three smaller bombs were assigned to McCallister's three coconspirators, all of whom had gained employment at The Arrington. We now know that their purpose was purely diversionary — to make us think the attack was a conventional one. The device in the trunk was transported to The Arrington in a hotel vehicle by one of the three coconspirators and placed in the suite reserved by McCallister.

"As you know, the presidents of the United States and Mexico were resident at the hotel for a conference and the signing of a treaty on security and immigration. Hundreds of other prominent people were either resident in the hotel or taking part in its grand-opening festivities. Two of the three smaller bombs were discovered by our teams before they could be detonated. The third was detonated in the Santa Monica Airport hangar, destroying the Caravan and killing its pilot and the third coconspirator. We believe this was the work of McCallister, who was covering his trail.

"McCallister then set the bomb to go off at eight-thirty in the evening, near the end of a concert in the Arrington Bowl, attended by fifteen hundred people. He left the bomb in the closet, as you see it, then was driven to LAX and boarded a flight for London.

"A magazine reporter who had met Mc-Callister and had had sex with him in his suite accidentally saw the trunk in question and that evening, when she heard that we had been searching for a large piece of luggage, informed Mr. Freeman and Special Agent Rifkin of the presence of the trunk in Mr. McCallister's suite. You all know what transpired after that. The following is what would have happened if the device had not been stopped from detonating."

The camera then zoomed out to an apparent altitude of several thousand feet, and an animated version of the nuclear explosion began.

8

Everyone started as the explosion of the device filled the screens. First there was an intense white light, followed by a fireball consuming the entire twenty-acre site of the hotel, and beyond, obliterating the Bel-Air neighborhood. This was coincident with a huge roar, shaking the speakers, and a visible shock wave that spread in all directions, destroying nearly all the buildings at UCLA, across Sunset Boulevard, and extending for miles farther. Fires broke out everywhere.

Everyone took a breath, but the event was not over. Up Stone Canyon, two city reservoir dams broke, and a high wall of water swept down the canyon, through the UCLA campus, and past Wilshire Boulevard.

The chief bomb technician's voice rose again. "The three and a half billion gallons of water in the two reservoirs would have had the effect of extinguishing most of the fires caused by the initial fireball."

The camera zoomed slowly upward, exhibiting the enormous swath of ruin left by the explosion.

"We estimate that more than a million people would have died in the first hour after the blast, and that as many as two million more would have died within ninety days from their injuries or from radiation sickness."

The camera continued to pull back, and the scar on the face of Southern California was still visible as the curvature of the earth came into view. The room went dark, and then the lights came up slowly.

The president spoke for the first time. "I want to thank all of you who had a part in finding and disabling this device before it could be set off. The entire country — indeed, the entire world — owes you all a debt of gratitude that can never be fully expressed. Indeed, it *will* never be expressed, since no one will know until most of us are dead. The public knowledge of this incident will be limited to the announcement that two bombs were discovered and disarmed on the site of the hotel and that one was set off by a coconspirator at Santa Monica Airport. After that, the airplane carrying McCallister to London was diverted to Kennedy Airport in New York, where his brother attempted to help him escape. Both were shot and killed by a CIA team dispatched to stop them. Dr. Kharl met his death a few hours later in Dubai, shot by a CIA sniper, who then made good his escape.

"As I'm sure you know, last year both houses of Congress passed a bill called the National Security Act, which I vetoed, because I felt that some parts of the bill were unconstitutional. Both houses then passed a revised version that I signed into law. One of the provisions of that act is that, by order of the president, information harmful to national security can be suppressed until fifty years after the death of that president. I view the nuclear nature of this event as falling under that provision of the act, and I am issuing an executive order, which you may read in the folders before you, invoking the National Security Act. Also in each folder is a statement that I wish signed by each of you present, saying that you are aware that the Act has been invoked, and that you swear to keep secret everything you have seen and heard here today, even to the extent of discussing them with each other, and also to keep secret your part in the events covered by the Act.

"I hope that each of you, having seen what the explosion of the device would have wrought, will agree that the country should not know these things for a long time to come. Later today I will address the nation and tell them of the bomb plot at The Arrington and how it was stopped. It is very likely that, after my broadcast, you may be contacted by members of the media for a statement. In that case, I ask you to refer all questions to the White House Press Office and to make no further comment.

"Now, with the pens provided, please sign your personal statements and give them to Tim Coleman."

Stone glanced at the brief statement and signed it. So did everyone else. Tim Coleman collected the statements.

"I want to thank you all for traveling here today and for your help in dealing with this very troubling situation," Will Lee said. "Good day to you all." He got up and left the room, followed by Tim Coleman.

Kate Lee spoke up. "Ladies and gentlemen, I am sure it has occurred to you that there was one other person present at The Arrington who possesses much of this knowledge. Kelli Keane, a reporter for *Vanity Fair,* has already agreed to keep her silence. Holly Barker spoke with her before the president decided to invoke the Act, so Holly will travel back to New York with a copy of the statement for her signature. She will be allowed to include a description of the search for the conventional bombs at the hotel but not to ask any of you for comment. Thank you all, and the helicopter is waiting for the New York contingent."

Everyone was very quiet during the helicopter ride back to New York.

Stone sat in the restaurant Patroon, sipping a drink and waiting for Holly to arrive. Ken Aretsky, the owner, joined him for a while but left as soon as Holly walked in. Stone ordered her a drink.

"How did it go?" Stone asked.

"How did what go?" Holly asked in return.

"Let me put it this way: Are you satisfied with the way your day's work went?"

"Entirely," Holly replied. She raised her glass. "Now we need never speak of this day again."

"I'll drink to that," Stone said, and he did.

9

Stone watched the president's address about events at The Arrington. It was brief enough to be delivered in its entirety during a time-out of a big football game being televised. His phone rang twice that evening, while he and Holly were in bed, and he did not answer either call.

The following morning Holly went to work at the Agency's East Side office, with the intention of returning to Stone's house that evening.

When Stone got downstairs to his office there was a stack of messages on his desk. He typed a short statement, printed it, and buzzed for Joan.

"Are they calling you about what happened at The Arrington?" she asked.

"Yes," Stone replied, handing her the statement. "Please call them back, read them this, then hang up."

Joan read the statement aloud: "Mr. Barrington has nothing to add to the president's address of last evening, nor will he at any later date. Please contact the White House Press Office with any questions you may have." Joan gathered up the message slips on his desk. "You could make a living as a PR guy for somebody who doesn't want to talk to the media." She went back to her desk.

In her borrowed office on the East Side, Holly called Tom Riley in London.

"Riley."

"It's Holly, calling from the New York office. I'm on a secure line."

"Good morning, Holly."

"What's new on Jasmine Shazaz?"

"Is this to do with the president's statement last night?"

"Yes. We believe she was present when the three bombs were assembled, and she may have had a hand in delivering them to L.A."

"Only three bombs?" Riley asked.

"What exactly do you mean, Tom?"

Riley was quiet for a moment. "Forget that."

"No, I want to know what you're referring to, so that this won't come up again."

"I haven't heard anything, if that's what you mean, but I dispatched the guy who took out Dr. Kharl, so I've just connected a few dots."

"Dr. Kharl designed and assembled the three bombs."

"Plastic explosives are not exactly in Dr. Kharl's line," Riley said.

"If you go back a few years, you'll find he had a very nice line in plastic explosives."

"That's the story, then?"

"Those are the facts, Tom. Any other questions?"

"No."

"Then please answer mine."

"MI-6 hit the Cheyne Walk house yesterday like a swarm of hornets, but all uniformed as painters, plumbers, and carpet cleaners, with their vehicles liveried as such. They were seen to have taken away two medium-sized safes and numerous file boxes. As a further cover, Hamish McCallister's solicitor was present to make things seem kosher."

"I see. Have you received any information from MI-6 that might be helpful to us?"

"They've been very quiet, and their chief of ops has not returned my phone call of this morning."

"Do we have any further information on Jasmine not associated with the house?"

"She went to a girls' school in Kent, then

to a Swiss finishing school. No university education that we know of."

"Any photographs?"

"One, when she was twelve and holding a hockey stick. We're aging it now."

"Please fax it to me in New York. Tom, you've no doubt heard details of how her two brothers were dealt with."

"I read Lance's report."

"You may take that as a model of how to proceed when we find her."

"Understood."

"I'll see if I can unearth anything from MI-6."

"I'll look forward to hearing from you, Holly."

Holly hung up, called Felicity Devonshire's direct line, identified herself, and asked for Architect. This time she was handled more gently and put through after half a minute on hold.

"Good afternoon, Holly, or is it morning where you are?"

"I'm calling from New York. Good afternoon. I've heard about your redecoration job on a house in Chelsea. Anything you can share with me? This is a secure line."

"It's quite a richly appointed residence," Felicity said. "Very nice artwork, probably in the value range of five to ten million pounds' worth. Hamish had very positive brokers' and bankers' statements in his safe. It seems he came into quite a lot when he turned twenty-one."

"Were there any photographs of his sister?"

"None, nor of his brother, though there were bedrooms that may have been used by both of them. We found some cosmetics in one bathroom. Everything, however, and I mean everything, had been wiped clean — no prints, no DNA."

"So, they had not planned to return there?"

"They might have returned, if their mission had been, ah, completely successful, and if they'd thought there was no trail to follow to them. In the circumstances, they might have been right."

"The president has issued an executive order under the new National Security Act, sealing everything except what he had to say in his address last evening."

"Yes, I saw that. You may take it that I am following his wishes, though I have no legal necessity of doing so. I have not reported to my masters what I have surmised from the bits and pieces of information gleaned during my stay in your country, nor shall I. I believe that's best for all."

"Thank you, Felicity. I will see that your position is known here in the places where it's important."

"I've no wish to be a loose cannon in this," Felicity said.

"The loose cannon, in this instance, is Jasmine Shazaz," Holly said. "Did you find anything at all in the house that might help us locate and identify her?"

"I'm afraid not. She may have a place of her own, but if so, we haven't found it."

"Do you think she's still in London?"

"If I were she, I would not wish to be traveling at this moment in time. I'd go to ground, perhaps for quite a while, until things are cool, even cold."

"This will not cool off for us, Felicity."

"Nor for us. Remember that our losses in this are greater than yours, but I understand your position completely, and I will see that any new knowledge of Jasmine reaches you."

"We are all grateful to you," Holly said. "Good-bye."

"Good-bye."

Holly believed everything Felicity had told her, and she felt better for it.

Architect hung up her phone and looked at the photograph of the beautiful young woman on her desk. "Circulate this," she

said to the man across from her. "Find her
and take her alive, if at all possible."

10

Holly found Stone in his study, and he poured them both a day's-end drink.

"God, I need this," Holly said, sinking some bourbon.

"Rough day?"

"A fairly fruitless day. It got rough when I had to issue some instructions."

"Dare I ask what instructions?"

"Don't ask. Suffice it to say that I gave someone permission — no, that's weaseling. I very nearly ordered someone to commit murder." She took another swig of the amber liquid.

"Don't you do that practically every day?"

Holly looked at him sharply, then realized he was just kidding. "Normally, no more than three or four times a week."

"You didn't see this sort of thing coming when you got your promotion?"

"When I worked for Lance he was a little protective of me, and he would give some orders to operatives himself."

"He was probably just eliminating you as a witness at some congressional hearing."

Holly laughed. "That's exactly what he was doing, but I also thought he didn't want me to get my hands too dirty, maybe because he thought I couldn't handle it."

"Was he right?"

"Oh, I'm handling it," Holly replied ruefully. "It didn't take me long to rationalize the whole thing."

"That's good self-protection."

"Maybe, but you know what I keep thinking? Somehow, during my meager childhood religious experience, I formed the view that when my life ended I would have to face God and . . . well, not confess the bad things I had done, because He would already know. I would just have to face Him knowing that He knows. That's pretty scary stuff, because at that point I wouldn't know where I was going to end up for all eternity."

"Scary stuff for a little girl," Stone agreed. "God will also know why you did what you did, and maybe he'll confirm your judgment, instead of drop-kicking you into hell."

"What an image! God coming down from his skybox and booting me between the goalposts, right into the flaming end zone seats!" She tossed off the rest of her drink and poured herself another. "Do you ever feel guilty about anything?" she asked.

Stone sighed. "When Arrington died, one of my first thoughts was the irrational feeling that I was somehow responsible."

"But you didn't do anything. . . ."

"I know, I know. I repeatedly worked my way back through the weeks before her death, and the worst I could come up with was that, if she hadn't married me, she wouldn't have died."

"As you say, irrational. I mean, she would have eventually dumped the guy, even if you weren't around, wouldn't she?"

Stone brightened. "Funny, I didn't think of that. Yes, she would have, surely."

"And then he probably would have done what he did anyway."

"That's an awful thought, but it makes me feel slightly less guilty."

"Well, your average shrink would probably tell you that a lot of people irrationally feel guilt when they lose somebody."

"Your average shrink? Have you ever talked to one of those?"

"Oh, I've talked to somebody like that once or twice a year since I've been with the Agency. The brass is always on the lookout for somebody who is about to bring an assault weapon to work. I mean, it's a lot more pressure than working at the post office, isn't it?"

"I can only guess."

"You know who I think never has a moment's guilt or a second thought about anything?"

"Who? Kate Lee?"

"Oh, no, Kate has a very active conscience — she's a Democrat, after all. No, I was talking about Felicity Devonshire."

"Well, Felicity is a pretty cool customer."

"When we were all in L.A. I had a chance to talk to her for the first time, and she was very warm and helpful. We were working out scenarios together."

"That's good, I guess."

"Yes, it is, and yet the whole time, I was wondering if she had her own agenda, which did not resemble mine in any way."

"Felicity is, in her way, impenetrable," Stone said.

"I hope that was unintentional humor," Holly said, laughing.

Stone laughed, too. "Well, all right, not *entirely* impenetrable."

"We talked on the phone today, and what she said was exactly what I wanted to hear, and yet, immediately after I hung up, I had the awful feeling that she had just lied to me."

Stone nodded. "I think Felicity would prefer to tell you the truth. I also think that if it were in her interests, or those of her service or government, she would not hesitate to lie to you or anyone else."

"Maybe that's part and parcel of what we both do," Holly said. "I suppose I've got to learn to do that."

11

Jasmine Shazaz sat on a bagged life raft in the rear of an old, unmarked American Huey helicopter and gazed out the open door at the terrain, lit by a rising sun. Her ears popped as the machine kept up with the elevation. They had been flying for a little over two hours. She turned to the Pakistani ISI agent on the bench next to her, leaned closer, and shouted, "Why would you have a life raft aboard a helicopter in a region with no water?"

The man shouted back, "Because if we have to ditch up here somewhere, we inflate the life raft, and it becomes a readymade tent, complete with emergency food and water — also flares and a radio."

"Oh."

"Yes, 'oh,' " he shouted back.

The chopper was suddenly closer to the ground, but it had not slowed. She looked more closely at the life raft and located the lanyard that inflated it, then she felt marginally better. The pitch of the rotors changed and the machine slowed. Moments later, the nose lifted, and the Huey settled to earth.

"Out!" the agent shouted.

Jasmine jumped to the ground, and she was immediately struck in the back by something soft. She turned and found a small duffel on the ground, along with her backpack.

The ISI agent was getting into a robe and turban. He bent, unzipped the duffel, removed a bundle of black cloth, and tossed it to her. "From here on, you wear the burka," he said.

"I'm not wearing that fucking thing!" she shouted at him.

The helicopter suddenly lifted off, revealing a couple of other men in native dress and a dozen mules, most of them heavily laden, on the other side of where the chopper had landed.

Jasmine looked at the mules incredulously. "And if you think I'm going to ride one of those things, you're completely crazy!"

The man's face changed, and he backhanded her, dumping her on her ass. "Now you listen to me, you stupid bitch: you will do whatever I tell you to do. If I tell you to strip, you'll strip, and if I tell you to fuck us all, you'll fuck us all. And if you don't do exactly what I tell you to do, I'll shoot you in the head and leave you here for the vultures. Do you understand?"

She stared at him blankly, unbelieving. "Do you know who I am?" she demanded, and regretted it immediately.

The ISI man unholstered his Beretta, racked the slide, and pointed it at her head.

"All right, all right," she muttered, getting to her feet. She held up the garment and tried to figure it out.

He snatched it away and threw it over her head, like a sack, and she managed to get her arms in the sleeves and settle it on her body. He grabbed the hood and pulled it over her head, until only her eyes could be seen. "There," he said, "that's very becoming. And by the way, I don't give a shit who you are. You are alone with three horny men in the middle of nowhere, and you will do as I say and quickly. Do you understand?"

"Yes," she said.

He pointed at a mule. "Get on that animal, and don't speak again unless you're spoken to."

Jasmine grabbed her backpack, slung it over the horn of the saddle, and managed to get aboard. The mule didn't seem to care one way or another. A moment later there was a jerk as the rope leading from her mule's bridle to the saddle of the mule ahead became taut.

Eleven hours later the little caravan wound along a steep, narrow trail. The air had become thinner, and the animals sucked and blew. They rounded a corner, and before them was a wide arch, covered by camouflage canvas. Everybody dismounted.

They had had only two breaks all day, and her bladder was bursting. "Where can I pee?" she asked one of the native men in Arabic.

He pointed. "Behind rock," he replied.

She ran around the big stone, hoisted the burka, dropped her jeans and squatted, leaning against the rock. When her stream made noise, the men on the other side of the rock laughed.

When she returned, the canvas had been pulled back, and the men and animals were inside a cave, lit by dim electric lights. The ISI agent grabbed her elbow and pointed at another woman in a burka. "Go with the women," he said. "You will be called when he is ready — maybe tomorrow."

"Maybe tomorrow? I've got to —" She stopped as he drew back his hand. "All right." She followed the woman along a passage and a moment later they emerged into a roundish cavern, perhaps twenty feet in diameter. Half a dozen women sat around a small fire that was lit in the middle, its smoke disappearing into the darkness above.

She was told she could take off the burka, then she was given a surprisingly good stew of lamb and vegetables, which she ate greedily. Then she was given a small pillow and a blanket and told to sleep. She had no trouble doing so.

She was shaken awake. Light was coming through a hole in the top of the cavern, and the other women were moving about. She was handed a bowl containing a hunk of bread and goat cheese. She ate the breakfast and washed it down with water from a canteen.

"You!" a man shouted.

She turned to find him pointing at her. "Put on the burka and come!"

She did as she was told and followed him back to the main passage and for perhaps a hundred paces, making several turns. She emerged into a well-lit room with carpets and pillows on the floor and several pieces of ornate furniture. Five men sat in a circle, eating. She was told to sit and be quiet.

Half an hour later four of the men left, and the fifth man beckoned her to come and sit before him. He seemed to be in his fifties, with a graying beard and broad shoulders.

"Listen to me," he said, and she nodded.

"Remove burka."

She pulled the garment over her head and smoothed her hair back.

"Stand there," he said, pointing at a white cloth hung on a nearby wall. "Brush your hair — look presentable."

She did so, tucking in her shirttail. A man appeared with a Polaroid camera and took her picture. When it developed, four images appeared and he took the photos away.

The man beckoned her to return to him, but he did not tell her to put on the burka again. "You are the sister of Ari and Mohammad, are you not?"

"I am."

"My condolences. I knew your father. My condolences for him, too."

"Thank you. My only wish from now on is to take revenge against British and American intelligence for their deaths. It would be my father's wish."

"I understand. It was important that I see you," he said, "before you continue your work. You are intelligent and, I suspect, very wily."

She smiled. "Thank you."

"You have good ideas for London."

"Thank you."

He rummaged in an ornate box next to him and came up with a sturdy brown envelope. He handed it to her. "Look inside."

She opened the envelope and removed a sheet of paper, to which a thin key was taped. On the paper was written the name and address of a London bank, a man's name, and a box number.

"You will go to the bank and ask for this man, then request to open your box. There will be money there, sufficient for your needs. When you have more ideas, more money will be in the box. You understand?"

"I understand."

The photographer returned and handed the man four booklets. He handed them to her.

"Here are passports with new names. You will use one to enter Britain, then destroy it. Use the others as necessary. Your contact remains the same. Now, put on the burka and go back the way you came."

She stood up and pulled the garment over her head, then she put the passports into her backpack and the key and instructions into the hip pocket of her jeans. She was led back the way she had come, and she emerged from the cave into bright sunlight. The ISI agent and another man were waiting for her, holding the mules, all now unladen.

"Get on," he said to her.

She got on.

As the sun was low in the sky, the helicopter appeared, guided by an electronic beacon held by the ISI agent. He waved the pilot in.

Three days later Jasmine opened the door to her London flat and let herself in. She ran a hot bath and stripped off her traveling clothes, tossing everything into her washing machine and starting it. Then she got a half-full bottle of scotch from the bar and settled into the tub, taking pulls from the bottle, hoping she would not drown.

12

Felicity Devonshire sat at her desk in her beautifully paneled and furnished office on the top floor of "The Circus," as the MI-6 building was called, even though they had moved from their old location in Cambridge Circus some years before. A green light went on over the door, and she pressed a button to unlock it.

A man entered with a file folder and handed it to her. "Architect, this was transmitted from Edinburgh Airport five minutes ago. Our facial recognition software caught it."

Felicity opened the folder and stared at a copy of a Syrian passport. The young woman in the photograph might well have been Jasmine Shazaz.

"She came in on a Syrian Air Force Dassault corporate jet from Damascus, also carrying two diplomats, duly registered with the Foreign Office. She walked away from the airplane before customs arrived, then went through immigration with no problems. She was carried on the airplane's manifest as a cultural assistant in the Syrian Embassy in London."

"So she did travel," Felicity said, using a magnifying glass on the passport photograph. "Tell our technical section, good job with the recognition software. Where did she go from there?"

"We thought perhaps the railway station, and we covered Glasgow and King's Cross, but nothing. Then we checked flight plans and found a small twin had departed Edinburgh ten minutes after she cleared customs, filed for London City Airport. It landed there an hour ago, dropped a female passenger, then took off again, filed for Edinburgh. As soon as it cleared London airspace the pilot canceled his flight plan. He could have landed anywhere."

"Don't bother searching for the airplane," Felicity said. "It will be a charter, and the pilot will be of no use to us."

"As you wish, Architect."

"So she's back in London," Felicity said. "I think we can expect havoc again soon." She handed him the copy of the passport. "Have this couriered to Tom Riley at the U.S. Embassy, for transmission to Holly

Barker at the Agency's New York facility. Actually, depending on how good their interception program is, she may already have it."

The man took the folder and left.

Holly arrived late at the New York office, still sleepy and a little sore from the previous night's recreational activity. There was a folder on her desk, and she opened it. There were two copies of the same passport, one intercepted, the other forwarded from MI-6. Holly looked at the photograph, then phoned Felicity Devonshire.

"Good afternoon, Holly."

At first Holly thought that was a needle, then she remembered the time difference. "Good afternoon, Felicity. Thank you for forwarding the passport to me. Is this a photograph of Jasmine Shazaz?"

"We believe so," Felicity replied. "She entered the UK at Edinburgh this morning on a diplomatic flight from Syria, carrying that Syrian passport."

"Was it a good document?"

"We don't have the original, but probably. A blank passport could have been provided by Syrian intelligence to anybody they trusted with it. I expect it's been shredded by now."

"Any news on where she might be?"

"Almost certainly in London."

"And what are the chances of picking her up?"

"It seems likely that she won't be walking the streets much, so I should say the chances are poor. We will probably hear from her next when something explodes, and what with our surveillance camera network in the city, we may have an opportunity then. We do have more news on the bomb at the Porsche agency."

"Please tell me."

"A fashionably dressed young woman entered the showroom carrying a large Hermès carrier bag, one of the bright orange ones, you know?"

"I know."

"She looked at a couple of cars on the showroom floor, and when the salesman left her for a moment, we believe she placed the carrier bag in the boot of a model 911 4S, then left the showroom. At any rate, she was gone by the time the man finished his call. The bomb went off about twenty minutes later as the foreign secretary's car drove by, almost certainly controlled by a cell phone from a parked car within sight of the showroom. The salesman was lucky — he had left the showroom floor to use the toilet."

81

"What measures are you taking to find her?"

"We're doing an all-hands-on-deck sweep, which means that every person associated with our service, MI-5, the Metropolitan Police, or the Foreign Office will be carrying the passport photograph, with instructions on what to do if she is spotted. Those persons who are armed are authorized to employ deadly force, if in their personal judgment it becomes necessary. Do your people have any need to speak with her? If she survives, we will be happy to turn her over."

"No," Holly said.

"I understand," Felicity replied. "We do wish to speak with her, albeit as briefly as possible, but after that we would not wish her to be available to visitors or other prisoners."

Or to anyone else, Holly thought. She thanked Felicity, hung up, and called Kate Lee.

"Good morning, Holly."

"Good morning, Director." Holly related her conversation with Felicity.

"I suppose we could call that progress," Kate said.

"I suppose."

"Do you think they'll actually turn her

over to us?"

"I declined the offer."

"Oh, good. I wouldn't like to make the next decision after that one."

"I was left with the impression that MI-6 and especially the Foreign Office are not especially interested in hearing what she has to say either."

"I expect we would see a brief news release from the FO saying that she was spotted, and after a brief exchange of fire, she expired of one or more gunshot wounds."

"That would be the best possible ending for everyone, except the lady herself," Holly said.

"Do we have the slightest reason to believe that she or her colleagues have the wherewithal to create another device?"

"Dr. Kharl is dead, and we know of no one outside a government facility who could accomplish that."

Kate sighed. "Then all we have to worry about is governments."

"The only conclusion we can draw at the moment is that this was a family cell comprised of mostly family members. It seems unlikely that any government, even Iran or North Korea, would wish to be involved in such an enterprise. The repercussions would be too great for them."

"Thank you, Holly. The president and I are going to Georgia for a few days. If you'd like some time in New York, then stay on."

"Thank you, ma'am. I'll be available at all times, of course."

"Of course. Good-bye, Holly."

"Good-bye, Director." Holly hung up. *Oh, good,* she thought, *some free New York time.*

13

Kelli Keane sat across the breakfast table from her boyfriend, James Rutledge, and stared over her newspaper at a row of kitchen cabinets.

"What's up with you?" Jim asked.

Kelli jerked back to reality. "What?"

"For the past couple of days you've been walking around in a daze, and once in a while you look really angry."

Kelli thought about how much she could tell him. "I'm trying to figure out a way around a promise I don't want to keep," she said, sipping her coffee, which had gone cold. She got up, threw it into the sink, and poured herself another cup. "More coffee?"

"Half a cup," Jim replied.

She poured it, then sat down again.

"Your eggs are getting cold."

She ate a few bites.

"I can't think of anything you promised me," Jim said. "We've never promised each other anything."

"Oh, it's not a promise to you."

"Then to whom?"

Kelli screwed up her forehead and tried to think of a way she could answer the question. "I think I may have promised not to tell anybody even that."

"Baby, are you in some kind of trouble?"

"In a way," she said. "I'm in the kind of trouble that a journalist gets into when she knows about something but can't write about it."

"Why can't you write about it?"

"Because I promised — I signed an agreement not to."

"A business agreement? With *Vanity Fair*?"

She shook her head. "No, it's bigger than that — it's bigger than anything, any story I've ever heard of."

"Well, let's see: bigger than the attack on Pearl Harbor?"

"Yeah, in its way."

"Bigger than nine-eleven?"

Kelli thought about that. "No, but it could have been."

"Are we talking terrorist attack here?"

"We're not talking," Kelli replied. "I can't do that."

"I haven't heard anything on the news or seen anything in the *Times* about anything like that."

"That's the thing — you won't see it or hear about it anywhere, because nobody can talk about it."

"Who comprises the category of 'nobody,' in this case?"

"Anybody who was there."

"There in L.A.? That's the only place you've been lately."

She nodded her head.

"Did something happen in L.A.?"

"Almost."

"I saw the president's TV address, and I read about the three bombs in the *Times*," Jim said. "But only one went off, and the only people killed were terrorists."

"That's accurate," Kelli said, "to a point."

"Was there another attempt on the president's life?"

"I can't talk about it anymore."

He put his hand on hers. "Kelli, whatever it is, it's eating you up. You might feel better if you talk about it. You know I'll keep your confidence."

"I know you would, Jim. But I thought I would, too, and here I am talking about it."

"Then do this: write it all down, pour out everything, then lock it in your safe and forget about it."

She frowned again. "You know, that might work."

"Well, I have to go to work," he said. "I've got to oversee the installation of some new lighting at High Cotton."

"I thought you were finished with that project."

"Yeah, well, when you think you're finished with a project, something always comes up. There have been some complaints about inadequate lighting in the programming department. People look at their brightly lit screens, then look at something on paper, and their eyes can't adjust quickly enough. The new fixtures have arrived, and we need to get them in today."

"You go ahead," Kelli said. "I've got to do some grocery shopping. Anything you need?"

"More bourbon," he said, "and more vodka."

"Okay, I'll call and have it delivered."

"And we're out of Parmesan cheese."

"Already on my list."

He stood up, held her face in his hands, and kissed her. "Feel better," he commanded, then he left.

Kelli slowly finished her breakfast and drank her coffee, then she went into her little workroom and sat down at her computer.

Last week in Los Angeles, during the Immi Gotham concert at the opening of The Arrington, a new hotel, a nuclear bomb came within three seconds of detonating. I was there. I saw it happen.

She wrote rapidly for an hour, editing as she went, then she saved the document, printed it, copied it to a thumb drive, put the hard copy and the drive into her safe and locked it, then deleted the original from her computer.

Then, unburdened, she called in the liquor order, stuck her wallet in a pocket in her jeans, and went grocery shopping.

14

Jasmine was awakened by the cell phone on her bedside table. She was disoriented for a moment, then she reached for it. It could be only one person. "Hello?"

"I think you should do some light grocery shopping this morning," he said.

"What?"

"After all, you've been away, your fridge must be empty."

"I need to sleep," she said.

"Sleep then. Do your shopping early this afternoon; take a walk, get some air. The park is nice this time of year."

"All right."

"Tell me what things you will buy."

She was hungover, but she tried to think. "Milk, bread, sliced beef for sandwiches, mayonnaise, eggs. And scotch."

"Famous Grouse all right?"

"Fine."

"Later." He hung up.

Jasmine rolled over and slept for another two hours, then she struggled out of bed and got into a hot shower, letting the water drum against the back of her neck to make the hangover go away. She toweled off, dried her shoulder-length hair with a large hair-dryer, then she looked for breakfast. Cereal, but no milk. She had it with water, then checked the kitchen clock: nearly one o'clock.

She got into a modest printed dress and flat walking shoes, then found a suitable scarf and covered her hair. She checked the mirror: without makeup she could pass for any one of fifty Muslim women on the street. She had chosen the neighborhood for that.

She let herself out of her building and walked two blocks to the Spar grocery, towing her shopping basket on wheels. She bought the things she needed, paid cash, then walked another block to her neighborhood's park. It was a well-shaded green space where mothers, many of them in Muslim dress, watched their children play and chatted among themselves.

Jasmine chose an out-of-the-way bench, parked her cart at the center, and sat at one end. She was still tired from her journey, and she hadn't had all the sleep she needed.

She resented being hauled out of bed on her first day back.

She could see a man walking slowly toward her, towing a shopping cart much like her own, dressed in a baggy suit and wearing a little embroidered cap, signifying his devoutness. He came slowly on, then parked his cart next to hers and sat down at the other end of the bench, took a newspaper from his coat pocket, and began to read it.

"How was your trip?" he asked, barely moving his lips.

"Rough," she said. "Two long days on a mule. I don't recommend it as a means of travel."

He chuckled. "I expect you have a sore ass, then."

"Don't ask."

"You recall our conversation of a while back when you mentioned three targets?"

"Yes."

"We think the third one would be appropriate at this time."

"Well, that's an escalation, isn't it?"

"Yes, and it's hard to escalate past a foreign minister."

"Somehow, that one is more satisfying," she said. "It might even make a difference, if we're lucky."

"We rely on planning, not luck," he said,

reprovingly.

"Of course."

"What will you need from us, besides matériel?"

"A black taxi," she said. "I was uncomfortable driving the car last time, and a taxi is the most anonymous of all vehicles."

"It will be done."

"What about the driver?" she asked.

He was quiet for a moment. "We must keep our numbers small. That is the way to remain safe."

"I agree," she said. "I'll need the package delivered. It must look good — a uniformed man in a liveried van, something like a DSL van."

"It will be done."

"I want another, larger device in the van. I'll need separate cell numbers for each."

"Interesting," he said.

"We can maximize results with collateral damage."

"I agree. When?"

"Five days. The parcel will be ready for collection at noon on the day and should be delivered at one P.M. Traffic will be good at the lunch hour."

"I have the list of cell phone numbers you gave me. Are they still good?"

"Yes."

"Dispose of the one you answered this morning and go to the second number. I'll call a day ahead of time to be sure everything is still on." He took a page from a notebook and slid it across the bench toward her. "This is a list of my cell numbers. The first and second may be used for the first and second devices. Call me only if absolutely necessary. Good luck." He rose, reached across his cart and took the handle of hers, then he walked back in the direction from which he had come.

Jasmine sat long enough to check the area for anyone following him or watching her. Finally, satisfied that she was unnoticed, she took the handle of the other shopping cart and towed it toward home. She noted that the grocery items she had ordered were the top layer in the cart. What was underneath was heavier.

She walked back to her flat, taking a circuitous route, checking reflections in shop windows and, occasionally, stopping to look at displays. It took her forty minutes to reach home.

She pulled the cart up the steps carefully, one at a time. When she was halfway up, the front door opened and a woman she didn't know stepped outside.

"That looks heavy," the woman said. "Let

me help."

"That's all right," Jasmine said. "I've got it."

"Let me get the door for you, then." The woman held it open and watched as she muscled the cart inside. She was English, mid-thirties, mousy hair, a plain coat, sensible shoes. Jasmine had never seen her in the building, and she was alarmed.

"We've just moved into the building," the woman said. "My name is Sarah."

"Welcome," Jasmine said. "You'll like the building."

A small car drew up outside. "Oh, there's my husband. Please excuse me."

"Thank you for your help," Jasmine said.

The woman got into the car and it drove away.

Jasmine left the cart in the hallway and ran to the rear of the building, looking out the window halfway up the stairs to the next floor. A woman and a child in the garden, a small dog in the woman's lap.

Jasmine ran back down the stairs and checked the street. A couple of cars passed without slowing down. A postman walked down the street, carrying his bag.

Jasmine let herself quickly into her flat, then checked all the windows overlooking the street. Nothing out of the ordinary.

Everything normal.

She took the cart into the kitchen, unloaded and put away the groceries, then wheeled the cart into the pantry and locked the door.

She checked the windows once more, then took off her dress and threw herself on the bed. Half an hour later, she was sleeping. An hour after that she woke with a sense of panic.

Something was wrong.

15

Felicity had just returned from her weekly lunch with the head of MI-5, which was responsible for domestic counterintelligence, when her phone buzzed. "Yes?"

"Architect, this is Mason. We may have gotten lucky. A woman who is employed as an agricultural analyst in the Foreign Office may have spotted Jasmine."

"When and where?"

"A little over an hour ago, in Notting Hill Gate. She and her husband moved into the building last week. She went home for lunch, and as she was going out again, she opened the door for a woman with a shopping cart: five-nine, pretty face, no makeup, wearing a Muslim headdress, unremarkable dress, sensible shoes. She believes the woman lives on the first floor of the building."

"Why didn't the FO woman call sooner?"

"She was delayed in traffic getting back to

her office, where she had left our flyer, and it took her a few minutes to find it and make the comparison. She called the duty officer, as requested on the flyer."

"So the woman she spotted is in the building now?"

"We have no reason to believe otherwise. Shall I raise the alarm?"

"Not yet. Get some people into the street, try and set up surveillance directly across from the building."

"I'll get the surveillance camera footage from the street immediately."

"Wait on that," Felicity said. "I don't want New Scotland Yard involved until we're ready to move, nor do I want MI-5 hearing about this until I tell them personally. First, I want photographic identification. If she leaves the building, I want her followed: team of twenty, six vehicles, greatest possible discretion. If she meets anyone, follow both. Do not intercept without my personal authorization. Call me when we have live surveillance. How long?"

"Twenty minutes."

"Then go!"

"Yes, Architect." Mason hung up.

It was probably a false alarm, Felicity thought, but still, she was excited.

■ ■ ■ ■

Jasmine looked at her cell list and dialed a number.

"Yes?"

"I'm blown. I want a black taxi *now* and two further vehicles, and I want this building watched, round the clock. How soon?"

"Stand by." He went off the line, then came back. "Taxi in twelve minutes," he said. "Clean up as best you can."

"That won't be necessary," she said, then hung up. She undressed and put on jeans and a sweater and pulled her hair back into a ponytail. She packed a carry-on bag and threw personal items into a leather tote bag. She went to her safe and removed the spare passports and cash and tossed them into the tote bag, then she went to the kitchen pantry, looked on a high shelf, and took down a shoe box containing five cell phones. She dumped four of them into the tote, then lifted the lid of the box in her shopping cart and connected the fifth phone, pulling off the sticky label containing the number. Ten minutes gone.

She exited the flat, leaving the door off the latch, and stood near the outside door, watching the street. Half a minute later, a black taxi came to a stop in the street and gave a short beep. The rear door on her side slid open. She opened the front door and, looking neither left nor right, walked in a leisurely fashion down the front steps and got into the cab. The driver pressed a button, and the door closed.

"First transfer in three minutes," the driver said, and the cab drove away at a normal pace.

As Jasmine's taxi made its first turn, Jasmine looked out the rear window and saw another black taxi enter the street. A few blocks later, her cab turned into a mews, rounded a corner, and stopped. A gray Ford sedan waited, its engine running. She got out of the cab and into the rear seat of the sedan, tossing her luggage in ahead of her.

"Get down," the driver said, then he drove out of the mews, made a turn, then more turns. Finally, she transferred to a Volkswagen Beetle driven by her contact.

"What happened?" he asked.

"Do you have anyone in the street yet?"

"A shopkeeper across the street a few doors down. What happened?"

"When I came home from my meeting, a woman I didn't know was leaving the building. She allowed the door to close to slow me down, then she introduced herself as Sarah and said that she and her husband had just moved into the building. Finally, she opened the door for me, and I went inside. Half an hour passed before it hit me: I saw a corner of a plastic ID card clipped to the collar of her blouse, under her jacket. Looked like a government ID, and she was too interested in me. That's when I called you."

Mason got out of the taxi with a female estate agent carrying a clipboard. They walked up the stairs of a house with a "Flat to Let" sign out front. Inside they walked up a flight and the woman took out a bunch of keys, found the correct one, and opened the door.

"I think you'll like the place," she said. "It's spacious, and the light is good."

Mason flashed a plastic ID at her. "Please sit down and be quiet. I'll only keep you a few minutes."

She looked surprised, but she sat down.

Mason pressed a speed dial number on his cell phone as he peeked through one side of the sheer curtains. "We got lucky," he said. "We're directly across the street, one floor up. The curtains are drawn in the flat. Is the team in place out back yet?

Good. Now bring in the SWAT team van, and block both ends of the street. Call me when everything is in place." He ended the connection, then turned to the estate agent.

"Is there a rear exit from this house?" he asked.

"Yes, it opens into a mews."

"Please leave at once by that exit, and walk quickly to the street behind and find a taxi. This is a matter of national security, and you are not to mention it to anyone. Do you understand?"

"I suppose so," she said.

His telephone rang. "Mason. Right. Go." He turned to the woman, who had gotten to her feet. "Too late. Please sit down again. This will be over shortly, then you can leave."

The woman sat down, and Mason watched through the curtains as a white van pulled up downstairs.

"Ring your shopkeeper," Jasmine said to her contact.

He did so and listened. His face changed, and he hung up. "They're in your street," he said to Jasmine. "A SWAT team is getting out of a van."

Jasmine dug a cell phone out of her tote bag and began to dial a number.

The assault squad ran up the steps of the house, six men in black uniforms with helmets, heavy armor vests, face protection, and automatic weapons. The front door was locked; a team member carrying a heavy horizontal sledge swung it at the lock, and the door came open. The six men crowded into the hallway.

"Flat door unlocked," one man said, trying the knob. The team flooded into the flat, weapons raised, shouting.

Jasmine pressed the last number.

As Mason watched from across the street, the front of the building blew out. He flung himself into the corner behind him as the window blew in, filling the room with glass and debris.

The estate agent began to rise from her seat, then she was struck by something heavy and sat down again. When Mason looked at her, most of her head was gone.

He pressed a speed dial number. "Major explosion at subject house. Many dead or wounded. Full immediate response!"

From down the street he heard the Klaxons of backup vehicles coming.

16

Holly finished the last of her to-do list and looked at the clock: later than she thought, and she was hungry. She packed her brief-case and shut it, then reached for the phone to call Stone. It rang.

"Holly Barker."

"It's Felicity Devonshire," she said, and she sounded weary and dejected.

"It's very late there," Holly said.

"We've had a major flap," Felicity replied. Then she gave Holly a brief account of what had happened.

"I'm sorry," Holly said. "Casualties?"

"Six of our people are dead, and one collateral."

"Jesus Christ!"

"Exactly. We're not sure what went wrong yet. We circulated the photo I sent you to a wide intra-government list, and one of them spotted her. We had people there in twenty minutes, but apparently Jasmine had gone.

And she left a very large surprise behind her."

"Anything at the site that might help?"

"We're still sifting through the rubble. We had to prop up the building. It's listing alarmingly and will have to come down. Fortunately, in the early afternoon the other occupants were at work."

"Why was your spotter there?"

"She and her husband had only recently moved in. They met there at lunch to look at some fabrics together, and it turned into a matinee, or she would have been back at work when Jasmine came home."

"How on earth did Jasmine know she had been spotted?"

"We're not sure, but when we interviewed the woman at the FO she had a ministry ID clipped to her collar. Jasmine might have spotted it."

"This is just going to get harder now, isn't it?"

"I'm afraid so."

"Can our London people be of any help?"

"No, now we have Special Branch involved, and, of course, our colleagues at MI-5 are on the job, furious that they weren't consulted before our raid. I'm putting out bureaucratic fires everywhere."

"You have my sympathy," Holly said. "I'll

see that the photo is circulated at the embassy. Who knows, somebody might spot her somewhere."

"That can't hurt, I suppose," Felicity said wearily.

"Get some sleep, Felicity, you'll have new ideas in the morning."

"I'm sleeping here tonight," Felicity said. "Talk to you later." She hung up.

Holly called Stone. "I'm sorry I didn't call you earlier, I've been at it all day. I hope you had dinner."

"I'm still waiting for you. Dinner's in the oven."

"I'll be there in ten minutes." She hung up and headed for the elevator.

"All right," Stone said, when he had dinner on the table and had opened a bottle of wine. "Tell me. You'll feel better."

"Well, since you're in the loop on this one I guess I'm on solid ground if you know more." She began with her visits to Kelli Keane, then went on to her conversations with Felicity Devonshire.

"So Jasmine is in the wind?"

"Absolutely. She could be anywhere by now."

Jasmine was, in fact, thirty miles up the

Thames from London in a secluded and comfortable riverside house.

"How long do I have this place?" she asked her contact, as she tossed her bags on the bed.

"The family is in Pakistan, visiting relatives. They're not due back for another month. They've called their housekeeper and told them that you are the doctor's cousin, and you're between flats and camping out here. She'll do for you."

"Thank God I don't have to go out. That's how the whole thing fell apart."

"It was a fluke, that's all. We've heard that the intelligence services circulated your passport photo widely in the ministries. No more headdresses. Dress fashionably."

"As fashionably as I can with what's in this bag," Jasmine said, opening the case and starting to put things away in the guest room dressing area.

"I'll get you some catalogues, if you want other things."

"Thank you, Habib. I have to go to bed now."

"Would you prefer to do so alone?"

"No, but I'm going to anyway." She pulled back the covers and started to undress.

Habib left and closed the door behind him.

■ ■ ■ ■

Kelli Keane was returning from a meeting with her editor at *Vanity Fair* when she stopped to pick up a bottle of wine for dinner. She left the wine shop and stepped into the street to do a bit of jaywalking, when a car she hadn't noticed whizzed by so close that the side mirror took the wine bottle out of her hand, smashing it into the street. She jumped back, terrified, then ran the rest of the way home.

"What's wrong?" Jim asked as she came through the door, tearing her coat off and flopping down in a chair.

"Somebody tried to run me down in the street," she said. "Drink, please."

Jim put some ice in a glass and poured her two ounces of bourbon. He put it into her hand and found it shaking. "What kind of car?"

"Dark — black, I think."

"Sedan? SUV?"

"SUV. I don't know what kind."

"Did you get a look at the plate?"

She shook her head and tugged at the drink. "I was too busy cowering between two cars. The windows were darkened, I remember that. It took a very good bottle of wine right out of my hand, a Mondavi Reserve Cabernet."

"That's tragic," Jim said, making her laugh. "Do you really think they were trying to hit you?"

"How could they come that close if they weren't trying?"

"I've got my famous meat loaf in the oven. It'll be ready in fifteen minutes or so."

"I'll just suck up bourbon until then," she said. "Maybe even another one after this."

"You won't get an argument from me," Jim said. "I know how much fun you are with a couple of drinks in you."

She squeezed his hand. "You could join me."

"I can do that," Jim said, pouring himself one and sitting next to her on the sofa.

She leaned close to his ear. "You know that thing I told you about?" she whispered.

"I know that thing you *didn't* tell me about," he whispered back.

"I think someone heard me not telling you about it. There's a tabloid that has a history of bugging *Vanity Fair* people to get inside info on what stories they're working on."

He leaned back and looked at her closely, but she pulled him back. "Do you know somebody who could come here and look for bugs?" she whispered.

He kissed her on the ear. "I know somebody who will know somebody who can do
that."

"Have them do it tomorrow, please."

17

Herbie Fisher was at his desk when Jim Rutledge called. "Good morning, Jim. Thanks for taking care of that lighting problem so quickly."

"All it took was twenty-seven desk lamps," Jim replied. "Herb, I need some advice."

"Sure. You want to come see me?"

"No, I just need a name."

"What sort of a name?"

"The sort who can come to my apartment and sweep it thoroughly for bugs."

"Do you have some reason to believe you're being bugged?"

"My girlfriend told me about something — No, strike that, she didn't tell me about something, but she intimated that she knew about something that happened in L.A. during the opening of The Arrington, that she couldn't tell me about. Then, last night, she was on the way home with a bottle of very good Cabernet in her hand when she was almost hit by a black SUV, darkened windows, traveling very fast. Took the wine right out of her hand."

"Who is your girlfriend?"

"Kelli Keane, magazine writer."

"Yeah, I remember her being out there."

"You were there, too?"

"Yes, my girl and I got there late, but we had a great time. Is Kelli talking about the three bombs that were intended for The Arrington?"

"No, that was reported in the press. There must have been something else."

"That's odd," Herbie said. "I think I was in a position to know if there was some other incident."

"Do you know somebody who can sweep the apartment?"

"As it happens, I do. She's my girlfriend, name of Harp O'Connor. She's a PI and does all sorts of security work."

"Could she come over? I'll be home all day, working on a project."

"Hang on a minute," Herbie said, and pressed the hold button. He speed-dialed Harp's cell.

"Hey, Herb."

"Hi, babe. A friend, architect by the name of James Rutledge, thinks his apartment may have been bugged. Can you do a sweep for him?"

"Where?"

Herbie gave her the address. "It's a loft downtown."

"I can be there about four this afternoon," she said.

"I'll tell him. Thanks, babe." He ended the call and pushed the other button. "Jim?"

"I'm here."

"Harp will be there around four o'clock."

"I'll look forward," Jim said. "Let's have dinner some night soon."

"Good idea. See ya." Herbie hung up, thought for a couple of minutes, then called Stone Barrington. Joan put him through.

"Morning, Herbert."

"Hey, Stone. Tell me, did something happen when we were at The Arrington? I mean, apart from the three bombs."

Stone was quiet for a moment. "Why do you ask?"

"I just got a call from Jim Rutledge, the architect, who lives with Kelli Keane." Herbie told him about her nearly being run down. "She thinks it's because she told Jim about something that happened at The Arrington."

"She told him about something that happened?"

"Well, no, she just intimated that something happened that she couldn't talk about. Next day, a black SUV with darkened windows nearly takes her out. She's scared."

"Nothing happened that I know about," Stone lied. "Will you let me know if you hear any further details about that?"

"Why?"

"I'd just like to know."

"Okay, Stone, if I hear more, I'll tell you. In the meantime, Harp is going over to Jim's place to sweep it." Herbie hung up. "Stone knows something," he said aloud to himself. "What's going on here?"

Stone called Holly on her personal cell phone.

"Hey, there," she said.

"Hey. You get back to Langley okay?"

"Yep. Choppered in about an hour ago."

"Tell me, did you have Kelli Keane's apartment wired for sound?"

Holly cleared her throat. "Why would you think that?"

"Because Kelli thinks that. She also thinks that somebody tried to run her down yesterday: a black SUV with dark windows. She wants her place swept for bugs, and her boyfriend called Herb Fisher for help."

"No, I haven't had her place bugged, and I haven't tried to have her killed. I'm

114

surprised you would ask me something like that."

"It's just that, after the conversation we had a few days ago, it occurred to me that you might have been referring to Kelli."

"No, I wasn't. Do you think she is becoming a security threat? I mean, I read her the riot act, and she signed the agreement."

"I don't know. I just hear that she's scared."

"Has she told her boyfriend something?"

"Apparently she just told him that something happened in L.A. that she couldn't talk about. Herb is sending his girlfriend, Harp O'Connor, over to Kelli's place to do a sweep."

"When?"

"At four this afternoon."

"Do me a big favor, Stone?"

"Sure."

"Call Herb back and tell him to ask Harp not to keep the appointment."

"For what reason?"

"Tell him it's no longer necessary."

"As you wish," Stone said. "Hope to see you soon?"

"Maybe sooner than you think," Holly said.

Jim Rutledge was working at his drawing

board at three o'clock when the downstairs bell rang. He picked up the phone and pressed the intercom button. "Yes?"

"Hi, Jim, this is Ted. Harp O'Connor asked me to come and see you."

"I'll buzz you in," Jim said, pressing a button.

A minute later, Jim opened the front door to find a short, pleasant-looking young man standing there, holding two toolboxes and an aluminum ladder hung over one shoulder.

"Hi, I'm Ted. Harp got an emergency call, so she asked me to take this one. We work together."

"Come in, Ted," Jim said. "What can I do to help?"

"Not a thing. Just do whatever you were doing, and I'll get to work."

"Okay," Jim said. He looked at his watch. "How long will you be?"

"A couple of hours. What time does your girlfriend get home?"

"She'll be a little late tonight, probably around seven."

"Good, I won't disturb her."

Jim went back to his drawing board, and Ted went to work, donning a pair of earphones and waving some sort of antenna around.

An hour later Jim finished his day's work, stood up, stretched, and went to find Ted. He was in the master bedroom with his equipment. "Ted, would you mind if I leave you here alone? I thought I'd catch a movie down the street."

"No problem," Ted replied.

"Just let yourself out when you're done. The door will lock itself."

"No problem."

Jim got his coat and left the apartment.

"No problem at all," Ted muttered to himself.

18

Holly was still at her desk at six-thirty when she got a phone call. "Holly Barker."

"Hi, Holly, it's Mike Theodore at the New York station."

"Hi, Mike."

"I visited the Rutledge and Keane apartment in New York, as requested."

"And what did you find, Mike?"

"I found that all the telephones had taps that would record anything said on the phone or in the apartment."

"That's interesting. What sort of equipment?"

"Over-the-counter, but good quality. The taps transmitted to a re-transmitter, and I found that on the roof, duct-taped inside an air vent. That unit could transmit eight to ten miles, maybe less in the city."

"Did you strip out the taps?"

"Yes. Rutledge came back from the movies as I was wrapping up, and I gave him all the equipment."

"What else did you do?"

"I installed six of our proprietary units, high-definition video and audio. For all practical purposes they're undetectable, at least by an ordinary tech or PI. If you want to take a look, I'll pipe it to your desk."

"My computer's on, go ahead." Holly watched as her screen went black, then came up again divided into six rectangles, each providing a look into a room.

"Got it?" Mike asked.

"Yes, it looks good."

"Write down this code." He read it slowly while she copied. "If you click on the button in the lower right-hand corner of each screen, you can operate the camera with the virtual joystick, zoom in or out, and control the volume."

Holly tried it. She clicked on the kitchen camera, and the image filled her whole screen. James Rutledge was at the stove, sautéing something. She zoomed in on the pan: shallots. She turned up the volume: sizzle. "Brilliant, Mike. Thank you so much."

"How long do you want the equipment left in place?"

"I'll let you know." Holly hung up and, as she watched, Kelli Keane entered the frame, still wearing her coat. They kissed, she shucked off the coat and left the screen. Holly switched back to the six-camera view and saw her hanging the coat in a closet near the front door. She then poured two drinks and took them back to the kitchen. Holly switched to the kitchen view.

"How was your day?" Rutledge asked.

"Run-of-the-mill," she said. "Just minor notes on a story. I fixed them on her computer. Did the scan lady show?"

"She sent somebody, who found that there were taps on all our phones."

"Shit!" Kelli said. "So they could listen to our calls?"

"Not only that, they could listen to anything we said in the apartment. The sound was transmitted to a black box on the roof, which could re-transmit it just about anywhere from midtown to the Battery. The equipment is on my desk."

Holly switched views and saw Kelli go to the desk and pick up one of the units, then she returned to the kitchen. Holly switched back.

"Did you ask him who uses that kind of gear?"

"Yeah, he says it's not government issue, FBI or CIA. You can buy it at those spy shops or on the Internet. Nothing to installing it. Can you think of anyone — not government — who would want to listen in on us?"

She seemed to think that over. "No, I can't. What about you?"

"Me? Who would want to listen in on an architect?"

"I don't know, a design freak, maybe?"

They both laughed.

"But," Kelli said, "who would want to run me over in the street?"

"Let's not make too much of that. It could have just been a bad driver. After all, you said you were about to jaywalk from between two cars."

"Maybe." She didn't sound convinced.

"Anybody try to kill you today?"

She slapped him on the back of the head. "You shut up!" They both laughed.

Holly called the New York station and asked for Mike Theodore.

"Yes, Holly?"

"I'm glad you're still there. How many black SUVs do we operate out of your station?"

"Six or seven, I think."

"Is there any record of their whereabouts yesterday, late afternoon, early evening?"

"Hang, and I'll check." He put her on

hold, then came back a moment later. "One on Long Island, one in Brooklyn, two in the garage all day, two in Manhattan, but never below Forty-second Street."

"Thank you, Mike, that's good to know." She hung up and looked back at the screen, then laughed. Kelli was sitting on the kitchen counter, and Rutledge was standing up, his pants around his ankles, fucking her. Holly switched off the images but realized she was aroused by what she had seen.

Later that night, in an office in midtown a man made a call.

"Yeah?"

"It's me. We're not getting transmissions from the Rutledge apartment."

"Equipment failure?"

"My equipment doesn't fail. I buy the best. I went down there and checked the transmitter on the roof: it was gone. I tested the system with another unit and got nothing. That means that the mikes were removed from all the phones in the apartment. Then I checked the recordings and this morning, Rutledge called somebody who said he would send down somebody to sweep the apartment. A man showed up later, and the last thing we recorded was Rutledge saying he was going to a movie.

After that, there were some noises, then the guy left the apartment. He must have found the rooftop transmitter, because we got nothing after that."

"What now?" the man asked.

"I bill you for the equipment, that's what, and it's going to be expensive."

"You told me it would be undetectable."

"Undetectable by Rutledge or his girlfriend. I said nobody but a pro could find it. The guy was a pro."

"Damn."

"You want me to break in again and re-bug the place?"

"I'd better speak to somebody before I can tell you to do that. Don't hurt me too bad on the equipment."

"I'll bill you the replacement cost. Tell your guy if you want me to go back in there, I'm going to have to do a different kind of job with different equipment, and it's going to be expensive. You got the low-cost option the first time." He hung up the phone and began typing out a bill.

19

Felicity Devonshire took her seat at the conference table in the room adjoining the offices of the newly appointed Foreign Minister, who pointedly did not sit next to her but across the table. Also present were Sir Trevor Peel-Jones, the head of MI-5, the intelligence service charged with domestic counterespionage and counterterrorism, and the cabinet member to whom he reported, the Home Secretary; Sir Robert Bacon, chief of the Metropolitan Police; and Chief Inspector Sir Evelyn Throckmorton, head of New Scotland Yard's Special Branch, which dealt with serious crimes.

"Now," the FM said, opening a file on the table before him, "we are here to discuss the actions of MI-6 in London yesterday. Six members of that service are dead, with an aggregate of five widows and nine children left to grieve their loss, and an estate agent, Susan Bell, who was present in a house across the street from the one in which the explosion took place. That house no longer exists, having been razed on the order of the local council."

He looked across the table at Felicity. "Architect," he said in an even tone, "what happened?"

Felicity took a breath and in her beautiful RADA/Oxonian accent, in measured cadences and without referring to notes, gave a detailed account of her orders to her people on the previous day and how they had been carried out. Her tone changed, becoming regretful only when she recited the names of the agents who had died. Finally, she said, "I have reviewed all of my actions and those of the people who acted on my orders, and I have determined that each of them acted in accordance with established procedures in such cases, and that the deaths occurred only because the suspect, Jasmine Shazaz, had left the house no more than five minutes earlier, leaving the bomb behind her. We believe that she set off the device by cell phone."

"Established procedures?" Sir Trevor practically spat. "There are no established procedures for MI-6 to conduct an armed raid on a house in the United Kingdom. Architect is aware that hers is a *foreign*

intelligence service, is she not?"

"Now, Trevor," the Home Secretary said, "let's give Architect an opportunity to address that issue before we go any further."

"Thank you, Home Secretary," Felicity replied coolly, "for pointing out the only point of this meeting. I took the actions I did because we had traced the recent arrival of this suspect from a *foreign* location and had advised the Home Office of her presence in the country. We did not establish any surveillance of the subject, nor did we advise MI-5 to do so, because we were not aware of her location. When we became aware, I had only *minutes* to react, and I took the decision to delay calling in MI-5 and Special Branch only because it would have taken them, based on past experience, some *hours* to react in a useful fashion. We had an opportunity to apprehend the al Qaeda operative responsible for the recent death of a foreign minister, and I placed the importance of that opportunity above bureaucratic cooperation."

Sir Trevor's voice became shriller. "I deeply resent the insinuation that involving the properly authorized organizations would have caused the opportunity to be missed."

"Sir Trevor," the FO said patiently, "I would point out that it would have been impossible for you to react in the time available, and if you had done so, it is your people who would be dead now, instead of those belonging to your sister service. It would seem that you have much for which to be grateful."

Sir Trevor took a breath but was stayed by the hand of the Home Secretary on his arm. "Trevor, Foreign Minister, I must say that, after Architect's very succinct and comprehensive presentation of the facts, I believe her actions to have been proper . . . in the circumstances. I know very well from her past cooperation with the Home Office and MI-5 that she is aware of the duties, obligations, and limitations placed upon her service by the government, and I believe that she had no intent to violate any of them. As far as the Home Office is concerned, this matter is closed."

"Thank you, Home Secretary," the foreign minister said. "In that case, this meeting is closed, and any notes or minutes taken are to be destroyed. All questions from the press or media are to be referred to the Public Information Officer of the Foreign Office." He closed the file before him, stood up, bowed briefly, and left the room. Before he turned down the hallway he looked back at Felicity and made a motion with his head, indicating that she should follow him.

Felicity gave the Home Secretary and Sir Trevor a polite nod, then headed down the hallway to the foreign minister's office.

He motioned her to a chair. "Do you need a drink?" he asked.

"Thank you, no, Foreign Minister," Felicity replied.

"Well, I do," he replied, swiveling his chair to a cupboard and pouring himself a glass of sherry. He swiveled back to face her. "I consider that, with the help of the Home Secretary, to whom I will now be indebted for eons to come, we have dodged a bullet. I assure you, Architect, that should any other such bullets come this way, you will take them."

"Of course, Foreign Minister. Is it your wish that I should henceforth defer to MI-5 in the matter of Jasmine Shazaz?"

"It is my wish that you should *appear* to defer to MI-5 in this matter, while pursuing Ms. Shazaz with all the resources at your disposal. It is this ministry that has been wounded, and I will not restrict the efforts of any member of it to put things right. I would suggest, however, that the next time a SWAT team is called for that it be provided by Special Branch, and that also

128

extends to any bomb disposal work necessary."

"I understand, Foreign Minister."

"I wish you to know that I have already authorized that the full death benefit available be immediately provided to the families of the fallen officers, and I have instructed an official of this ministry to offer a generous gratuity to the surviving husband of the estate agent."

"Thank you most kindly, Foreign Minister."

"Please let me know if there is anything else I can do for your people." He stood and offered her his hand. "Good day."

She shook it. "Good day, Foreign Minister." She left his office and took the lift down to the garage, where her car and driver awaited. She got in, rested her head on the back of her seat, and breathed slowly and deeply all the way back to the Circus. Then she got out of the car and went back to work.

Thirty miles up the Thames, Jasmine sat in a comfortable chair, not watching the cricket match that was on television. The rear doorbell rang, and she got up to answer it.

A look through the peephole revealed

129

Habib standing on the back steps, and she opened the door to him.

He walked into the house wheeling a nylon suitcase behind him. "Your replacement explosive device, madam," he said.

20

The president and first lady alit from Marine One at the White House helicopter pad and were escorted by a pair of uniformed Secret Service agents into the building and upstairs to the family residence. Their luggage followed shortly, and a valet unpacked for them.

"Drink?" Kate asked as they entered their living room.

"Have I ever replied in the negative to that question at this time of day?" Will asked.

"No, but a simple 'yes' would have gotten you a drink faster." She poured them both one and took her time about delivering his.

"Point taken," Will said sheepishly.

"Point scored," she said, sitting down beside him. "I have a question."

"Fire away," he said, taking a gulp of his bourbon.

"May I take your sexual performance over the weekend as a harbinger of things to come during our retirement?"

"You may," he replied, clinking glasses, then kissing her. "And you may have noticed that my enthusiasm increases when we are in Georgia."

"I have noticed that," she said, "which is why I haven't insisted on a retirement residence in New York or Malibu."

"Suppose I told you that I believe my enthusiasm in Georgia is due to the distance from Washington, rather than something in the Meriwether County water?"

"Then I would insist on an additional retirement residence."

"In New York or Malibu?"

"Both."

Will laughed heartily. "I'm not sure that the income from my memoirs will cover two additional houses."

"You forget that I will be publishing my memoirs, too."

"All right," he said, "tell you what: I'll buy the New York residence, and you buy Malibu."

"T'other way 'round," she replied. "Your memoirs will bring more than mine, and Malibu is more expensive than New York."

"I don't know if that's true," Will said. "After all, you've got your CIA background."

"Most of which I can't write about."

"Oh, all right, I'll buy the Malibu place."

"Deal," she said.

"I'm not sure how the Secret Service is going to take this news," Will said. "I think they were counting on an easy life in the rural South."

"I don't think they'll have any trouble finding volunteers for Manhattan or Malibu."

"Good point."

Kate's handbag rang. She rummaged around in it for a moment, then, in frustration, emptied it onto the coffee table and found her cell phone moving across the shiny surface, vibrating.

"Yes?" she said, when she had cornered it against her compact.

"Director, it's Holly Barker."

"Hello, Holly. Has anyone ever put that to music?"

"No, but someone once wrote dirty lyrics to the tune of 'Hello Dolly' for my fortieth birthday party."

"I suppose that was inevitable."

"Apparently so."

"What have you to report?"

"I have screwed the lid down a little tighter on Kelli Keane. One of our New York people has equipped James Rutledge's apartment for video and sound."

"Do they lead lives of quiet desperation?"

"Hardly, ma'am. You wouldn't believe their sex life."

Kate roared with laughter. "Be sure and copy me on the sauciest bits."

"Certainly, ma'am."

"Has the woman spilled any beans yet?"

"Not on our tapes, but our man discovered that the place had already been bugged with audio devices before he got there. Unfortunately, we were not privy to what was heard before our equipment arrived."

"Any way to find out?"

"We can try to find out who purchased the previous equipment."

"Please do. I worry about the New York station having too little to do."

"It does seem very quiet whenever I'm there," Holly admitted.

"It occurs to me that you always seem happiest when you return from New York. Is there something there that entertains you?"

"You might say that," Holly replied.

"It occurs to me that you might manage this particular task more easily if you were at the New York station for a time."

"Your suggestion is my command," Holly said. "I'll leave tomorrow morning."

"And we may reach you at Stone Barrington's number?"

"Nice try, ma'am. I'll be reachable on my cell at all times."

"Enjoy yourself, then, and let me know if there's any change in the position of the lid on Ms. Keane."

"Certainly, ma'am," Holly replied. "Have a nice evening."

Kate hung up.

"How's that thing going?" Will asked.

"Holly appears to have a grip on the problem. So far, she's getting video from the apartment of a lot of bedroom action."

Will laughed. "So that's what you were talking about: seeing the 'saucy bits.' "

"It'll have to do for fun, until we can have more non-D.C. sex," she replied.

Holly called Stone.

"Hello, there," Stone said. "Am I hallucinating, or did we just talk moments ago?"

"You're not hallucinating. Think you can put up with me for another little while?"

"Funny, I was just thinking about putting up with you. How long do I get to do that?"

"I might stretch it into a week, unless something terrible happens somewhere in the world."

"Something terrible is always happening somewhere in the world."

"I mean somewhere in the world that requires my attention."

"That would be right here in this house."

"You say the nicest things."

"I do the nicest things, too."

"And I will look forward to that."

"Is your trip to do with our Ms. Keane?"

"Yes, but that's only an excuse to come."

"Any excuse will do," Stone said. "Let yourself in whenever you arrive, and I'll book a table somewhere sumptuous for dinner tomorrow evening."

"I thought *I* was going to be dinner."

"You are going to be a very rich dessert."

21

Herbie Fisher and Harp O'Connor were having dinner in the back room at P.J. Clarke's, a regular hangout for them since they had met there at the bar.

"Herb," Harp said, "how come you set me up for that sweep at Jim Rutledge's place, then pulled me off?"

"I'm sorry. Did I mess up your day?" He began to think about lying to her.

"Just answer my question."

Herbie made up his mind. If he started lying to her about the little stuff, it would soon spread to bigger stuff. "Stone Barrington asked me to pull you off."

Harp chewed in silence for a moment. "Do you know why?"

"No, I don't," Herbie replied.

"You didn't ask?"

"No, I didn't."

"I find that very peculiar."

"It's like this, baby: there are only two or

three people in the world that I trust completely, and Stone is one of them." He almost stopped there but caught himself. "You are another."

"I know why you trust me, Herb, but why do you trust Stone?"

"Because I have a long experience with him, and he has always been worthy of my trust."

"Before I met you and heard you talk about him, I'd heard that he was just some kind of sleazy fixer for Woodman & Weld."

"Stone likes to say that he handled cases for Woodman & Weld that the firm didn't want to be seen to be handling. That doesn't mean they were sleazy cases, just sensitive ones."

"Well, I have to admit that he went way up in my opinion when we were in L.A. and found ourselves having drinks and dinner with the president of the United States. How'd that come about?"

"Well, I've never had a substantive conversation about that with Stone, but I've picked up fragments here and there."

"Gimme some fragments, I *love* fragments. I make my living on fragments."

"Did you meet Holly Barker at that dinner?"

"Tall, auburn hair, good body?"

"That's the one. Holly works at the CIA, for the director. The first lady?"

"I got that. I read the papers when she got the appointment."

"Holly got Stone and Dino involved with some CIA business or other down in the islands a few years back. I've never known what it was about. I think Stone met the president about that time. Then there was that thing when he and Dino went to Washington at the president's request a year or two ago to investigate some old murders that a friend of the president's, now dead, had been accused of."

"Yeah, that one made the papers."

"That's it."

"That's not all that much."

"It's all I know," Herbie said. "I don't think Stone would like it if you asked him about it."

"Okay, next time I have a couple too many, I'll try not to ask him. What I want to know is why he wouldn't want me to sweep Rutledge's apartment."

"Like I said, I trust Stone, and he asked me."

"Maybe he — or Holly Barker — didn't want me to find any bugs."

"And why would they want that?"

"Maybe because the Agency planted them?"

"Jim Rutledge is an architect and interior designer, who used to be the executive art director for *Architectural Digest*. Why would the Agency want to bug his apartment?"

"Maybe because he lives with that Kelli Keane person, who is a journalist? We met her in L.A., too."

"That's right, we did. But the CIA isn't allowed to operate domestically — that's FBI territory."

"And you believe the Agency sticks to that? Come on, Herb."

"I don't have any personal knowledge that they don't stick to it."

"Did something happen when we were at The Arrington that I don't know about?"

"If you don't know about it, it's because I don't know about it either."

"So we're both in the dark?"

"I don't even know if there's any dark," Herbie said.

"In my experience, which is extensive for a woman who is as young as I am, there's always dark."

"You, young lady, are a cynic."

"There's a lot to be cynical about," Harp replied. "Is Jim Rutledge your client?"

140

"Yes. I set up his business structure for him."

"So you have attorney-client privilege with him?"

"Yes, but so far, you haven't intruded on that."

"Are you friends?"

"We have a cordial personal relationship."

"Could you set up a dinner with us and him and Ms. Keane?"

"Funny you should mention that, we discussed getting together."

"Well, let's do it," Harp said. "I'd like to get a closer look at Ms. Keane."

"Okay, I'll call him." Herbie waved at a waiter for the check. "Maybe I'll invite Stone, too."

"That would be good. I'd like to get to know him better. Is he seeing somebody?"

"Always," Herbie said.

22

Jasmine Shazaz sat at a desk by the window in a small waiting room at the personnel office of the United States State Department, across the street from the United States Embassy. She could see down into Upper Grosvenor Street, which ran off the south side of Grosvenor Square, where the embassy, a massive building of reinforced concrete with a giant eagle out front, sat facing the square.

From where she sat, slowly filling out a job application for a position as an interpreter, she could see down into the intersection of Upper Grosvenor Street with Burnes Street, which ran behind the embassy, crossing Culross Street, ending at Upper Brook Street.

"How are you coming with the application?" the receptionist asked.

"I want to get everything just right," Jasmine said.

"Please be as quick as you can," the woman said. "We close in an hour, at five, and if you don't have your first interview before then, you'll have to come back another day."

"I won't be much longer," Jasmine replied, watching the DSL delivery van pull to a stop at Burnes Street, which was blocked by a steel security barrier.

The driver leaned out his window and shouted at the armed police constable at the barrier. "Hey, mate, I've got a delivery at the embassy, rear door. How do you want to handle this?"

"I'll take it," the cop said.

"It weighs over a hundred pounds," the driver replied. "I'll need to hand-truck it in there."

"Who is the addressee?" the policeman asked.

The driver picked up a clipboard and flipped a page. "Bloke name of Thomas Riley, cultural attaché, from an address in Langley, Virginia, U S of A. And he has to sign for it personally."

"Hang about," the policeman replied. He pressed the push-to-talk button on the microphone under the epaulet on his left shoulder. "Security, this is PC Bartlett at

143

the Burnes Street barrier. I've got a DSL delivery of a heavy parcel for Mr. Thomas Riley, Cultural Affairs. Needs to come in on a hand truck, and he has to have Riley's signature."

"Where's it shipped from?" a voice came back.

"A place called Langley, in Virginia, USA."

"Stand by."

"I've called it in," he said to the driver. "They'll get back to me."

"I can't block this street all day," the driver said.

"Don't get your knickers in a twist."

His radio came alive. "Okay, have the man hand-truck it to the rear entrance. Mr. Riley will meet him there and sign for it."

"Roger." The cop turned back to the driver. "Unload it here and follow me with the hand truck," he said. "The bomb squad will want a good look at you. Just leave the van there."

"Whatever you say, mate." The driver got out of the van and went to the rear. He unlocked the door and operated the power tailgate that lowered the crate to the street. He got the lip of the hand truck under an edge and rocked it back onto the wheels. By the time he got it to the barrier, the copper had slid it back enough for him to wheel it through. The officer slid it shut behind him.

"All right, follow me," he said to the deliveryman. The copper led the way to a steel door, where he rang a bell. A long moment later the door slid open, and the deliveryman could see another barrier a few feet inside. "Bring it right in and set it down," the copper said.

The deliveryman did as he was told, and the door slid closed behind him. "Oy," he said. "How'm I gonna get out?"

"Wait till it's signed for, and we'll let you out."

Two U.S. Marines in fatigues came toward them, preceded by an eager black Labrador retriever.

Another Marine at the next barrier picked up a phone and spoke into it, then hung up. "Riley will be right down."

"Are you gonna need me to roll it somewhere?" the deliveryman asked.

"No, you can just leave it there," the copper replied. "I'll get our hand truck."

Jasmine got up from the table, taking the application with her. "Excuse me," she said to the receptionist. "Where is the ladies' room?"

"Just around the corner to your left," the woman said.

"I'll be right back." Jasmine stepped out the door and walked toward the emergency staircase, which had a large exit sign above it, well lit. As she did, her cell phone began to vibrate in her jacket pocket, the signal that all was ready. She checked to be sure she had enough bars, then pressed a speed dial button on her phone, put it back into her pocket, opened the door to the stairs, and started to run down them. She descended two floors, stepped outside into South Audley Street, where a black taxi waited for her, its engine running. She got into the vehicle, and as it rolled away the bomb inside the rear door of the embassy detonated with a huge roar.

Protected by the buildings on the west side of the street, the taxi drove down to Mount Street and took a right. Now sirens could be heard. The taxi got to Park Lane and made a left turn, filtering into traffic. The driver edged into the right lane and turned into Hyde Park behind the Duke of Wellington's house, now a museum. They were all the way to South Kensington before the first emergency vehicles made it into Grosvenor Square.

The taxi stopped, Jasmine got out, removed a roller suitcase from the cab, and looked at her watch as she headed for the

London Underground entrance. The second bomb, the one on a timer in the DHL van, would be going off at this moment.

Ten minutes later she was speeding west, toward Heathrow Airport. Once there, she would take a taxi back to her new home on the Thames, along with the rolling suitcase, looking like any other Heathrow arrival.

Holly Barker got out of the chopper at the East Side Heliport and into the black SUV waiting for her. As she did, her cell phone went off, and she dug it out of her pocket. "Holly Barker."

"It's Scotty," her secretary said. "Where are you?"

"I just arrived in New York."

"Can you get in touch with the director? Her cell phone didn't answer. I know she got back last night, but she's not in the office yet."

"Yes, I can."

"Tell her this: a large bomb has detonated at the rear door of the London embassy, and there are many casualties. Hang on," she said, "other line." She came back after a moment. "A second bomb has gone off in a delivery van parked in North Grosvenor Street, probably on a timer. That's all I've got. I'll call you when there's more."

"I'm headed for the East Side station. Call me on a secure line there." Holly hung up and pressed the speed dial button for Kate Lee's cell phone. It rang five times before it was answered.

"Yes?"

"It's Holly. Where are you, Director?"

"In my car, on the way to Langley."

"Tell your driver to take an alternate route on surface roads and to proceed with caution," Holly said. "There's bad news from London."

23

The phone was ringing in the office as Holly hurried into the room, and she grabbed it. "Holly Barker."

"It's very bad," the director said. "There are at least thirty casualties, including Tom Riley."

"How did they get to Tom?" Holly asked, knowing that his office was several floors up.

"For some reason, he went down to sign for a package, which was the bomb. A second bomb went off in the delivery van, which was sitting in Upper Grosvenor Street, doing a lot of damage to the offices across the way."

"What can I do to help?"

"Ed Marvin, the deputy London station chief, had coronary bypass surgery yesterday and won't be back at work for at least six weeks, and Lance is in Hawaii at a Pacific Rim security conference, so you're now acting London station chief, until we can sort things out. An airplane will be waiting for you at Teterboro at eight P.M., and the chopper will take you out there at seven-thirty. You'll be met at London City Airport, and the Connaught will have a suite for you. Call me from the embassy on my cell as soon as you've assessed the situation. Don't worry about the time difference."

"Yes, ma'am."

"And, Holly, I'm sorry about your New York visit. Since Stone is a consultant to us, you can take him along, if you can talk him into it."

"I'll order him to come," Holly said.

"Good luck." The director hung up.

Holly dialed Stone's number, and Joan put her through to her boss.

"Have you heard about London?" Holly asked.

"I'm watching it on CNN right now," Stone replied.

"The director has ordered me to London, and she said I could take you along. Meet me at the East Side Heliport at seven-thirty."

Stone hesitated for only a moment. "I'll be there," he said.

Holly hung up and dialed the direct line to the London station chief's office.

"Yes?" A woman's voice.

"This is Assistant Director Holly Barker. Who is this?"

"I'm Ann Tinney, Tom Riley's assistant."

"I was very sorry to hear of Tom's death," Holly said.

"Thank you, Ms. Barker."

"Since Ed Marvin is in the hospital, and Lance Cabot is at a conference in Hawaii, the director has asked me to act as station chief until the situation is stabilized."

"I understand. When will you arrive?"

"Tomorrow morning. Please have key staff standing by for a meeting. I'll want an update on the casualty list and the damage, and then I'll want individual briefings from each desk chief."

"Of course."

"I'm at the New York station now, but I'll leave here in two hours. You can reach me on the airplane through the switchboard at Langley, if there's anything further to report."

"I understand."

"Thank you, Ann. I'll see you tomorrow morning." Holly hung up and logged into the Agency's mainframe computer from the station at her desk. She entered her password, then went into the personnel database and called up the list of London's station key staff and began reading their files. Twice during the next two hours Ann Tinney called from London and gave her updates. It was getting worse.

Holly and Stone had dinner on the Gulfstream G-450, and she managed to get a few hours of sleep before the flight attendant woke her in time to shower and change before landing.

When she was back in her seat, the flight attendant came back to brief her. "There's fog in London," she said, "but the pilot says the ceiling is eight hundred feet, so we shouldn't have a problem landing. The approach is steeper than at most airports and the runway shorter, so be prepared for that. An embassy car will be waiting on the ramp for you." She went back to the front of the airplane and buckled in.

"Excuse me," Stone said, rising from his seat. "I want to watch this approach from the jump seat." He went forward.

Holly could see nothing but gray outside the windows. As the flight attendant had warned, the approach was steep, and they broke out of the clouds in time to get a good look at the Thames. On touchdown, the reverse thrusters came on, and the pilot braked hard. A moment later they were turning off the runway and onto a ramp.

Stone came out of the cockpit grinning. "That was exciting," he said.

The attendant opened the door, and they descended to the ramp, where a car was waiting that looked much like the presidential limousine.

"They've sent the ambassador's car," Holly said, when they were inside. "This is embarrassing." The door shut with a soft clunk, and they could barely hear the sound of an aircraft taking off from the runway.

"I could get used to this," Stone said, stretching his legs.

"I can't believe they sent this car," Holly said.

"In the circumstances," Stone said, "I think they wanted you transported in something bombproof."

"Oh, I hadn't thought of that."

She dropped off Stone and her luggage at the Connaught, then the car continued the short distance to the embassy. She was met by two Marine guards at a side entrance on Upper Brook Street, and whisked to the top floor.

"The ambassador wants to see you," one of the guards said as the elevator stopped. A moment later she was in a large office being greeted by a gray-haired, well-tailored gentleman.

"Ms. Barker," he said, offering his hand. "I'm Ambassador Walters. I just wanted to say hello before you go down to the Agency floor, and extend my condolences for the death of Tom Riley. He was a good man, and I relied on him completely."

"Thank you, Ambassador," Holly replied. "I'm grateful for your condolences, and I'll pass them on to the director when we speak."

She was escorted back to the elevator by the two Marines, then down a couple of floors. They emerged from the elevator into a small lobby. A receptionist stood and indicated a steel door, which was electronically opened. After that it was just offices, like everywhere else.

She was escorted to a large conference room, where Ann Tinney, a tall, handsome woman in her fifties, introduced her to a dozen men and women around the table, then offered her the chair at the head.

"Good morning," Holly said. "I'm glad to meet you all, and I want to tell you how sorry I am for your terrible loss of Tom Riley. I knew him pretty well and admired him.

"The director has appointed me acting station chief until things become more . . . regular. I understand that I'm not Tom Riley, and I'm going to need the help of each of you to get through this."

Holly turned to Ann. "Now, I'd like to be briefed on exactly what happened, the casualties, and the damage. I'll have to report to the director shortly, and I want to be prepared."

24

Ann Tinney operated the video equipment from the seat next to Holly. "We've put together clips from a dozen surveillance cameras to give you a graphic idea of what happened." She brought up the first video.

"Here we have the DSL van, stolen, of course, pulling up to the barrier at the Upper Grosvenor Street end of Burnes Street. You'll hear the police constable call in the driver's request to deliver a large box, addressed to Tom Riley, with a return address of Langley." The audio played, and the barrier was removed so that the crate could be wheeled to the back door.

"Stop," Holly said.

Ann stopped the footage.

"There's something I don't understand," Holly said. "Why would Tom leave his office and go downstairs to receive a shipment, even if it was from Langley?"

"We're embarrassed by that," Ann replied,

"but as you heard, the delivery required his signature, and since it was from Langley, Tom thought it important enough to go downstairs himself. There is nothing in our security protocol that would prevent him from signing personally."

"Let's get the protocol amended immediately to cover that situation."

"Certainly. Shall I continue?"

"Yes, please."

The view from a camera inside the rear door. "As you see, the steel security doors are opened to admit the shipment. The driver is now in a room built of reinforced concrete with steel doors that we consider bombproof."

"Unless the bomb is inside the room," Holly said. "Amend the protocol to check with the shipping company and the putative sender before admitting any package to the building."

"Yes, ma'am."

"Holly will do, for all of you. Continue, please."

"Here's a view of Tom entering the room, looking curious. He takes the clipboard from the driver and examines it." The audio came on.

"Get this crate out of here and secure the room!" Tom shouted.

"The dog had not signaled, but apparently something about the clipboard aroused Tom's suspicions, and he acted without delay. We see the rear doors opening, and then . . ."

The video went to one frame at a time: Tom turned and shouted at the Marines, the crate exploded, and both video and audio ended.

"Tom was seconds away from having the crate outside and the room secured when the bomb detonated. There was no action on the part of the deliveryman, so it would have been detonated by cell phone or radio," Ann said. "Now we see the explosion from outside, from a camera on the State Department building across Upper Grosvenor Street, in slow motion."

The force of the blast blew a police constable out of the building and across Burnes Street, where his body collided with a neighboring building. A Metropolitan Police car parked in Burnes Street was blown into that building, as well.

"Now we switch to another camera in Upper Grosvenor three minutes and twelve seconds later," Ann said.

The DSL van exploded with a ferocity as great as the first bomb. Cars and pedestrians were blown about and shattered.

"Jesus Christ," Holly said involuntarily. "What was the death toll?"

"In the downstairs room, Tom, the police constable, two Marines who were there to examine the crate, plus another Marine at the desk, and the Labrador retriever sniffer dog were killed instantly. The room contained the blast, as it was designed to do, but the doors were open, so there was residual damage outside. A police constable in the patrol car was killed, and four people in the building across Burnes Street were seriously injured. Thirty-two other people were killed when the second bomb detonated — pedestrians, people in passing cars. The van partially blocked Upper Grosvenor, so traffic was bumper to bumper. Four of the dead were in the State Department personnel office across Upper Grosvenor. Eighteen other people either in the street, in cars, or in that building were injured, four of them seriously. The rest was from flying glass and shrapnel. That's it."

Holly heaved a deep sigh. "All right. I have to report to the director now, and after that I'll see the desk chiefs, one at a time, please, in Tom's office, to get an overview of current operations in your various purviews."

Ann Tinney stood up. "I'll show you to Tom's office." They left the conference

159

room and started down the hall. "All of Tom's personal effects have been cleared from the room, so you needn't worry about disturbing anything there. It will be your office while you're here."

"Thank you," Holly said. She was shown into a large corner office with unremarkable furniture, including a round conference table in a corner. Opaque window shades prevented photographing from outside. "Please excuse me, Ann, while I phone the director."

"Of course." Ann left the room and closed the door behind her.

Holly picked up the phone, then put it down again. She had never seen anything so horrific, and she needed a minute or two and some deep breaths to get control of herself. She looked at her watch, which displayed the two relevant time zones: it was four A.M. in Washington. She dialed Kate Lee's cell number.

Kate answered on the second ring. "Holly? I've been expecting your call."

"I'm sorry to wake you. I've just had a full briefing on the two bombs, with both video and audio." She recounted what she had seen.

"Have them transfer that presentation to both the White House situation room and to my office at Langley," Kate said calmly.

"Yes, ma'am."

"Can you explain to me why Tom went down to sign for the crate?"

"He thought it was from you. The security protocol doesn't cover such an incident, and I've instructed that it be amended immediately."

"It was a stupid mistake," Kate said.

"From what I've seen, it was the only mistake anyone made, and even that wasn't against protocol. The room where the bomb went off performed as designed."

"It's a very great disaster," Kate said.

"How long do you think it's going to take to get a new station chief in place?" Holly asked.

"I spoke to Lance last night. He's on his way home now, and he'll have a list of candidates when he gets to Langley later this morning. Have you been briefed by the desk chiefs yet?"

"No, that's next on my schedule."

"One or two of them may be on Lance's list of candidates, so I'll be especially interested in your assessment of them as individuals."

"I'll try and have that for you by the end of the day here," Holly said.

"The president made a brief appearance

in the press room last night to announce the bare bones of what happened. After he's viewed the security camera footage, he'll have a press conference to outline what happened."

"I'll get the footage transmitted as quickly as possible," Holly said.

"Good-bye, then. We'll talk later today." Kate hung up.

Holly called in Ann Tinney and gave her instructions on transmitting the footage, along with her commentary. "I'll start seeing the desk chiefs now," Holly said.

25

Holly got to the Connaught just after nine P.M. and was shown to the suite. She had called Stone when she was on her way, and he took her in his arms.

"It must have been a very bad day," he said.

"I just cannot explain to you how bad," she replied. "Before this is over we'll have forty dead — more than half of them collateral damage, complete innocents."

He put her down in a comfortable chair, gave her a drink, then sat on the ottoman and rubbed her feet.

"That's the first good thing to happen today," she said, tugging at the drink.

"I've ordered dinner," Stone said. "It will be here in a few minutes."

"Oh, thank you. I had half a cup of soup early this afternoon. It was back-to-back briefings, and I hope I can retain half of what I learned. I certainly have a new

163

respect for what the London station chief does. He has all of Europe under his purview. The only good thing is that everything is being smartly handled and operated. It's a tribute to Tom Riley and Ed Marvin."

"Who's Marvin?"

"Deputy station chief. Had bypass surgery two days ago, out for a couple of months, probably."

The doorbell rang, and Stone let in the waiter with his tray table. He opened the wine and tasted it while the table was being set up. The waiter carved the roast chicken Stone had ordered and served the vegetables, then retreated.

"God, this looks wonderful," Holly said. "I'm glad you ordered something simple."

"Did you talk to the director?"

"This morning. I owe her a call, but I'll wait until she wakes up tomorrow. I woke her at four A.M. this morning."

"The papers are over there," Stone said, nodding toward the coffee table. "The bombing is wall-to-wall — on TV, too. Did you speak with Felicity?"

"Not yet. I've just been trying to absorb what the staff here told me. I think it's unlikely that she knows anything I don't."

"You never know," Stone said. "It's her 'patch,' as the Brits like to say."

"I'll call her in the morning. What did you do today?"

"I visited my tailor, or rather, the tailor who has replaced my tailor. Doug Hayward died three years ago, and his shop was bought by another, larger shop. Most of Doug's people have been let go. It was depressing."

"Poor baby. I wish I had had that good a day."

Stone laughed. "I wasn't making comparisons. How long do you think you'll have to stay?"

"Three or four days, maybe a week. If I know Lance, he'll be here as soon as he can. Of course, he had to travel all the way from Japan, so he'll be terminally jet-lagged. I think I've found a possible replacement for Tom Riley, so I'll recommend him. Lance may have other ideas, who knows? He was supposed to have replaced Dick Stone here."

Stone's cousin had been London station chief, until he was promoted to deputy director for operations. He died before he could take that office, and Lance had moved up.

"Yes. He'll probably want someone who can replace him at Langley, if he gets Kate's job when she retires."

"Any ideas about who the bombers were?"

"Likely al Qaeda," Holly replied. "I'm meeting with the Metropolitan Police tomorrow morning to find out what they've learned."

"Maybe I'll have some shoes made tomorrow, or buy a hat," Stone said.

Holly began laughing. "You sound like the little woman on a business trip with her husband."

"That's pretty much my role, isn't it?"

"Tell you what, just to make you feel necessary, why don't you join my meeting with Special Branch tomorrow morning? You have all the clearances you need, and you're a paid consultant to the Agency, so you might as well earn your keep. You could have some insights into how their investigation is going, too."

"Love to. You think Jasmine Shazaz did this?"

"I'm trying not to make that a supposition in order to keep a clear head, but probably."

"There has to be a major manhunt on for her."

"Oddly, no. Not yet, anyway. So far, they've limited their hunt to circulating her photograph to employees of several ministries. That's how they nearly got her the first time and lost six men doing it."

"I read the account in the *Times,*" Stone said. "They'll have to go all out in their search now. For what it's worth, that's what I would have done when the foreign minister bought it down the street."

"Was that near here?"

"Maybe a hundred yards. The Porsche dealership is just before you get to Berkeley Square."

"I suspect that Special Branch will agree with you on that. I hear they felt excluded when Felicity sent in her own team."

"I expect so."

"Stone, let's try not to get embroiled in their politics, shall we?"

"I'll just listen," Stone said.

26

The following morning a car, less grand than the ambassador's, called for Holly at the Connaught, and Stone accompanied her to the American Embassy.

"It's only a short walk," Stone said, getting into the rear seat with Holly.

"They don't want me on the sidewalks," Holly said.

"Ah."

"Yes."

They arrived on the floor of the London station, where Stone was presented with a laminated ID card with his photograph on it, apparently from Agency records.

"You can hang on to the ID card," Holly said. "It might come in useful someday."

Stone looked carefully at the card: the letters CIA were printed large, background for the printed information. They would make the first impression if the card were flashed at someone. "I'm 'deputy assistant director'?" Stone asked, reading from the card.

"I thought it sounded better than 'consultant,' " Holly replied.

"Let's see, that makes me your deputy, doesn't it?"

"I thought you'd notice that."

They were taken down the hall to Tom Riley's office, and Holly introduced Stone to Ann Tinney, who took their coats and brought a pot of coffee. "The others are due shortly," Ann said, then left them alone.

"Who's coming?" Stone asked.

"A contingent from Special Branch," Holly replied. "I don't know whom they're sending."

Stone poured them some coffee, but before they could take a sip, Ann was back with two gentlemen, one tall, slender, with an impressive military mustache and beautifully cut clothes, the other shorter and heftier, wearing an off-the-peg suit and a crafty look.

Ann made the introductions: "Assistant Director Holly Barker, her deputy, Stone Barrington. May I present Chief Inspector Sir Evelyn Throckmorton and Inspector Harry Tate?"

Throckmorton managed a warm smile with his handshake. "Hello, Stone, it's a very long time since we met."

"Sir Evelyn," Stone said. "Good to see you."

"You know each other?" Holly asked incredulously.

"Sir Evelyn, or rather, just plain Inspector Throckmorton as he then was, once investigated me for something — I forget what."

Sir Evelyn stroked his mustache with a knuckle. "Let's see," he said, narrowing his eyes. "I believe it was murder."

"Fortunately, I was innocent," Stone said.

"I don't believe we ever actually determined that as a fact," Sir Evelyn said, and got a laugh from everyone.

"I'll tell you later," Stone said to Holly.

Holly waved them all to seats, and Ann poured coffee for them. "Gentlemen, thank you for coming. Naturally, we're very anxious to hear what you've learned over the past forty-eight hours."

"Harry," Sir Evelyn said, "give our friends the short version."

"I'll skip the damage and the casualties," Tate said, with a Cockney accent that had been mostly trained away by his advancing rank over the years, "since you've already heard about that. We're very short of living witnesses, since almost everybody who was close enough to see the explosions was injured, or died either immediately or shortly thereafter. You've seen the surveillance footage?"

Holly nodded. "Yes, in great detail."

"Then you know pretty much what we know. Our people are out there now, shaking down every Arab, Afghani, and Pakistani snitch we have, and combing the files on every nascent terrorist group. It always takes more time than we mean it to."

"I'd hoped for more," Holly said, half-absently.

"I'm *so* sorry we don't *have* more," Sir Evelyn said, with more than a trace of British irony.

"I didn't mean to be critical, Sir Evelyn," Holly said. "It's just that we're not equipped here — or for that matter, authorized — to conduct the kind of investigation that you're conducting."

"Quite," Sir Evelyn replied, with an air that said anyone could place any meaning he or she liked on that word.

"Are there any living witnesses at all?" Stone asked.

"One," Harry Tate replied. "She had a good view and as a result was badly injured, but I hope she can give us something. I'm seeing her in hospital when we finish here."

"Has the name of Jasmine Shazaz come

up?" Holly asked.

"I thought you'd ask that," Sir Evelyn replied, "as did your counterparts at MI-6. The short answer is: not yet, but nobody will be shocked if we hear that name spoken."

"I would be shocked if it weren't spoken," Holly said. "She's got to be at the root of this."

Stone spoke up. "If you'll forgive me, Sir Evelyn, I wonder why I didn't see her name and photograph in this morning's papers. Are you not conducting an all-out hunt for her?"

"We are," Sir Evelyn replied, "but rather quietly. Every police officer, taxi driver, airport porter, ticket agent, security officer, and milk deliveryman has her photograph, but we're not ready to have her splashed all over the tabloids just yet. We think, at this point, that a general alarm would produce more false sightings and phantom leads than we could deal with, and would waste a great deal of our time. We're better off concentrating our search on the places I've mentioned."

"Perhaps so," Stone said.

"She's not walking the streets and dining in restaurants," Harry Tate said. "She's gone to ground, and she won't pop out again until she's ready for another bombing."

"Naturally," Sir Evelyn said, "we've taken every possible precaution at the sort of targets she'd be interested in." He looked regretful. "I'm sorry we didn't include American targets."

"Quite," Holly said, gaining a clamped jaw from Sir Evelyn.

"Well," the chief inspector said, "if there's nothing else at the moment, I'd better let Inspector Tate go and see our witness." The two Englishmen stood, and Holly and Stone stood with them.

"Would it be inconvenient if I came along?" Stone asked. "Merely as an observer, of course."

The two policemen exchanged a glance and Sir Evelyn nodded almost imperceptibly.

"Glad to have you, Mr. Barrington," Tate said. "I have a car waiting downstairs."

Stone sat in the rear of the unmarked police car and stole a sideways glace at Harry Tate. "Been at this a long time, Inspector?"

"Call me Harry," he replied.

"And I'm Stone."

"I heard about you from Sir Evelyn," Tate said. "He remembers you fondly from your past meetings."

Stone laughed. "I'm sure that's not quite true."

"To answer your question, Stone, I've been at it for nigh onto thirty years, and it's nice to get out of the bloody office."

The car stopped at the entrance to a large hospital.

27

The hospital was much like any of its large New York City counterparts: everybody in green scrubs, patients on gurneys in the hallways, nurses looking overworked. They were met by a doctor, a Sikh, bearded, with a large turban. He introduced himself, and his English was impeccable.

"Mrs. Margaret Meyers-Selby is an American woman, thirty-seven years old, five feet six inches tall, nine stone three pounds," he reported, as if they were med students doing rounds. "She was standing in front of a window when a large explosion took place in the street and has suffered the loss of her left eye and sustained a large head wound, as well as many cuts made by flying glass. You will note that, except for her eye, most of her wounds are not bandaged, as the result would give her the appearance of a mummy. She is remarkably well, considering what happened to her, and you will find her articulate."

"Thank you," Harry Tate replied. He led Stone into the room, which was curtained off into four cubicles, Mrs. Meyers-Selby's by the window, which overlooked a rear utility area of the hospital. The woman sat up in bed, reading a magazine with her remaining eye, and the sight of her face was horrific. Seemingly dozens of wounds, some of them two or three inches long, had been sutured, painted with iodine, and left bare. Her face had swelled to what Stone imagined must be twice its normal size, and he thought that once she might have been very pretty.

She looked up from her magazine. "Don't worry, gentlemen," she said, "it's nothing a little pancake makeup won't fix."

Stone avoided laughing and pulled up two chairs. Harry introduced them. "We'd like to ask some questions, if you're up to it," he said.

"I appreciate the break in the otherwise constant boredom," she said. "If you don't like Cockney soap operas, soccer, or cricket, there's nothing to watch on TV."

"Can you please relate to us what happened, as best you can remember?" Harry asked.

"I remember every bit of it," she replied

176

in a clear American accent, "and I'll be happy to. I had received an applicant for a job as a translator," she said, "and she was sitting at the window, filling out the application form and taking her own sweet time about it. She excused herself to go to the ladies', and perhaps a minute later there was an awful explosion outside somewhere. I went to the window to see what the hell had happened and saw a police car upside down in Burnes Street, and what appeared to be a policeman's body, hanging on a wrought-iron fence.

"I stared dumbly at it for perhaps half a minute, then I went back to my desk, got an outside line, and called nine-nine-nine. I told them who I was and what had happened and requested every available ambulance and policeman to come to the scene at once. I could already hear sirens. After I had told the officer everything twice, I hung up and went back to the window. At that moment, the window blew into my face, and I flew backward. I may have been out for a few seconds, but then I managed to get to my feet and walked through a lot of glass back to the window and looked out. It was carnage, pure and simple. There were the remains of cars, taxis, and trucks everywhere, and bodies and pieces of bodies strewn all over the place. I stood there until the EMTs got to my floor, then they put me on a stretcher and got me to the hospital. I didn't even realize at first that I was blind in one eye. Sorry, missing an eye. I didn't know that, either."

"When you were looking out the window," Harry asked, "did you see any people walking about?"

"You must be joking. Anybody in the block was maimed and dead or dying, even those who had been running toward the blast when it occurred."

"Thank you, Mrs. Meyers-Selby," Harry said. "I don't think we need trouble you any further." He looked at Stone. "Unless you have something, Mr. Barrington."

Stone reached into an inside coat pocket, removed a sheet of paper, unfolded it, and handed it to her. "Have you ever seen this person before?"

"Yes," Mrs. Meyers-Selby said unhesitatingly. "She is the woman who was filling out the employment application and who left my office a minute or so before the first explosion."

"What sort of accent did she have?" Stone asked.

"BBC English."

"And what language did she wish to be

178

hired to translate?"

"Arabic and Urdu."

"Do you remember the name she used?"

"Khan," Mrs. Meyers-Selby replied, and spelled it. "I don't remember a first name."

"How was she dressed?"

"Like a British office worker — dark skirt, Liberty print blouse, and gray cardigan. She had a Burberry raincoat, looked like a knockoff. She left it in my office when she went to the ladies'."

"Thank you, Mrs. Meyers-Selby," Stone said. "I hope you have a speedy recovery."

"I could go back to work now, if anybody could stand to look at me," she replied, sounding sad for the first time.

Harry thanked her again, and they made their exit. "I want that raincoat," he said, taking out a cell phone.

Jasmine sat in the back of the van and waited while Habib took some packages from it and handed them to a uniformed pilot at the cargo door of a medium-sized jet airplane. When he had finished, he got a plastic shopping bag from his car and brought it to her. "Inside is a kind of money vest. I have removed your funds from the deposit box in the London bank, changed them into more convenient currency, and placed the notes in the vest which, worn under your clothes, will give you the appearance of having gained weight.

"You will be met at the airport and driven to a safe house, changing cars along the way. Our people there have already located some possible targets for you to consider in the city, and we would like an attack as soon as possible. Any questions?"

"Yes. Why am I being moved?"

"Jasmine, you are too hot to remain in Britain. *Everybody* is searching for you."

"Oh, all right."

He looked around, then waved her out of the van, up the aluminum ladder, and into the airplane, tossing in her roller suitcase behind her. Habib unhooked the ladder and tossed it into the airplane, then, with a wave, closed the door.

"This way," said the pilot, who was a young, skinny East Asian in black trousers, white shirt with epaulets, and a black, gold-trimmed hat. He led her forward to the cockpit and settled her into a seat immediately behind and between the pilot's and copilot's seats. Another young man in uniform was in the left seat, running through a checklist. Shortly, he started one engine, then the other. The copilot handed Jasmine a headset.

"You can listen if you want to. The chat with the controllers gets boring, but we'll have some music later." He handed her two folded newspapers. "Here's the *Times* and the *Sun,* depending on your tastes. We already have our clearance, and if there's no delay for takeoff we should be landing in Reykjavik in about two and a half hours."

The airplane started to taxi, and Jasmine strapped herself in and opened the *Times.* Big headlines and photographs of the bombing scene. She involuntarily smiled.

The copilot looked at her curiously, then turned around.

She put on her headset. "Southampton Tower, AeroCargo 3 ready to taxi to the active runway."

"AeroCargo 3, Southampton Tower, taxi to runway 18 without delay. We've got light aircraft traffic on a ten-mile final, so we can squeeze you in ahead of him."

"Roger, Southampton Tower, taxiing to 18, no delay."

Two minutes later they were over the English Channel, making a right turn to the north.

The copilot turned and looked at her. "You should have more than two hours to make your flight out of Reykjavik," he said, "and the weather forecast is for a smooth flight."

"Thank you," Jasmine said, and returned to her newspaper. Later in the flight, she undressed and donned the money vest.

28

Harry Tate dropped Stone off at the embassy, then drove away. Stone flashed his new ID at the Marine guards, and, after carefully examining it, they escorted him to the elevator and pressed the floor button for him.

"Don't get off at any other floor or you'll be shot," the young Marine said with a straight face.

Stone rode upstairs and was admitted to the sealed floor. He walked into the station chief's office and found a strange man sitting behind the desk. He was disheveled, had a couple of days' beard growth, and had the hollow eyes of the seriously jet-lagged. "Hello, Lance," Stone said.

"Stone," Lance replied. "Sit down. Holly will be back in a minute."

"How was Tokyo?" Stone asked.

"Charming," Lance replied. "The flight here was something else — an air force transport, two stops for refueling."

Holly walked into the office. "Oh, you're back. How was the witness?"

"Remarkable," Stone said, tossing the photo of Jasmine on the desk. "She identified this woman as being in her office, applying for the job of a translator of Arabic and Urdu, who left to go to the ladies' a minute before the first explosion."

"Got her!" Holly said.

"Have you? Where?"

"I mean, you've pinned the bombing on her."

"Well, yes, the witness confirmed your supposition. What are you going to do about it?"

"I assume Harry Tate was with you, so there's no need to inform Special Branch. What else should I do?"

"How about circulating that photograph to the known world? Or are we worried about the tabloids?"

Holly turned to Lance. "Your thoughts?"

"Wire it to the FBI and let them notify all the other agencies," Lance replied. "Come to think of it, I wouldn't be surprised to learn that she has left the country. We'll see where she pops up next."

"Just follow the explosions," Stone said.

"You seem a little off, Stone," Holly said.

"I've just seen a formerly beautiful woman who has lost an eye and had her face permanently altered by flying glass. It didn't improve my mood."

"Did Harry show her this photo, or did you?" Lance asked.

"I did, after Harry had finished questioning her and was ready to leave."

"Did Harry seem surprised that you showed it to her, or that she identified Jasmine?"

"No."

"I didn't think so," Lance said.

"Throckmorton told us he hasn't issued a general alarm for her, either — just distributed the photo to a whole lot of functionaries, including milkmen."

"I wondered about that," Holly said.

"A smart move," Lance said. "Thousands of milkmen will be delivering to all sorts of obscure addresses in the UK. They might well spot her in a housedress, watching soap operas on the tube."

"If you say so," Stone said.

"At any rate," Lance continued, "I think Throckmorton has indicated to us that he does not want the British public at large to know that the two most horrific bombings in London since the IRA attacks during the seventies have been carried out in his city by a mere slip of a girl."

Ann Tinney came into the room. "Architect is here," she said. She stepped back and allowed Felicity Devonshire to enter, dressed in a tailored suit of Scottish tweed, her red hair tucked up in a bun.

Stone and Lance stood up and shook her hand; Stone planted a kiss on her cheek.

Ann Tinney spoke up again. "By the way, I've just had a call from the State Department personnel office across the street. Harry Tate showed up there a couple of minutes ago and confiscated a woman's Burberry raincoat found in the rubble of the office. I thought you'd like to know." She closed the door.

"Raincoat?" Lance asked.

"Jasmine's," Stone replied. "The witness mentioned it."

"Oh, let Special Branch paw the thing for a couple of days," Felicity said. "Maybe they'll come up with a strand of DNA or a receipt with Jasmine's home address on it. If they do, the rest of us will hear about it in a week or two."

"You're in fine form, Felicity," Stone said, smiling. "What have you been up to?"

"I've been stacking sandbags in front of my service's building all day," Felicity replied dryly.

"Personally?" Lance asked.

"Figuratively. I reckon we're next. I'm traveling in the FO's upholstered version of a Bentley armored personnel carrier. I don't like hunkering down and waiting — I'd prefer to be combing the hedgerows for her myself."

"I can just see that," Stone said.

"What are you lot doing, then?" she asked. "And is it possible to obtain a cup of tea in this establishment that didn't come in a bag?"

As if on cue, Ann Tinney opened the door and entered with a tray containing a china teapot and matching cups. "May I pour for everyone?"

"Almost everyone," Lance said.

Ann poured.

Felicity tasted her tea cautiously. "Ah, Fortnum's Earl Grey," she said. "Thank you, Mummy."

"To answer your first question," Lance said, "we're doing pretty much what you're doing."

"Stacking sandbags?"

"A little late for that, but we're under the same investigative strictures your service is."

"I dislike strictures," Felicity said.

"Well, Architect, we're flattered that

you've ventured out onto the streets to come and see us," Lance said. "Now, what may the government of the United States do for you?"

"Let your worldwide network of stations know that Jasmine Shazaz is in the wind. That's what I've ordered done, and we could use the help."

"You think she's left the country?" Holly asked.

"It's what I would do," Felicity replied. "It's better than living in a spider hole."

"Any thoughts on where she might have gone?"

"Langley, Virginia, I expect."

Holly and Lance looked at each other.

"She's out for revenge, isn't she?" Felicity asked, rhetorically. "And she's made a start. She's too hot to continue here. She'll be looking for something to blow up where she's not expected."

"Thank you for that wisdom, Architect," Lance said. "Now I'm going to curl up on that sofa over there and sleep for an hour, then I will start acting on Holly's personnel recommendations. They were very good, Holly, I am in complete agreement. Now you and Stone go to a matinee, or something."

"Good idea," Holly said.

"The Gulfstream is arriving tonight with a couple of other people. The two of you can take it back to New York tomorrow morning."

"I'm relieved, then?"

"No, *I'm* relieved that you've done a good job here, and I thank you. Felicity, you can curl up on the sofa with me, if you like," Lance said by way of dismissal.

"Thank you, but there's a tank waiting for me downstairs," Felicity replied. "Holly, can I drop you and Stone anywhere?"

"Is there room in this vehicle?" Holly asked.

"Oh, dear, yes."

"Then we'd be grateful for a lift to the Connaught."

"Done."

Lance hit the sofa, and the others left.

Stone and Holly got out of the armored Bentley at the Connaught and bade Felicity good-bye.

"Did Lance say we should go to a matinee?" Holly asked.

"Perhaps he meant that we should *have* a matinee," Stone replied, ushering her quickly through the lobby.

"Good idea," Holly replied.

29

Jasmine stood before an immigration officer at Kennedy Airport in New York and handed him her British passport, along with her most brilliant smile.

The young man's eyes lingered on her face, then flicked to the passport and back. "The purpose of your visit, Ms. Avery?"

"Pure pleasure," Jasmine replied, turning her smile into a laugh.

He stamped the passport and handed it back to her. "Welcome to New York, Ms. Avery. I hope you enjoy your visit."

"Oh, I will," Jasmine said, accepting the passport and tucking it into her bag. She rolled her bag through customs, unimpeded, and emerged into a large hall where a group of livery drivers held up signs with their passengers' names on them, one for Ms. Avery. She handed the handle of her case to the driver and walked alongside him.

"Good flight?"

"Perfectly normal," Jasmine replied.

"Our people will be glad to see you."

"And I, them," she said.

She settled in the rear of the black Lincoln sedan and took a deep breath. She had slept remarkably well in first class and felt ready to greet the day.

Two changes of cars later she was set down at the curb in front of a pretty town house in the West Forties with geraniums growing in window boxes.

"Basement," her driver said, then drove away.

She walked down a few steps, towing her case, then under the main stairs to a heavy door and rang the bell. She looked up into a surveillance camera and smiled.

A moment later the door opened and a fashionably dressed, middle-aged man in a business suit let her in. "Welcome to New York," he said. "I am Habib."

"Everybody's Habib," she said, then rolled her case into the apartment. It was bigger than she had thought it would be, with a large living room with a dining alcove. Habib took her case and rolled it to the rear of the apartment, showing her the bedroom.

"Do you need to sleep?" he asked.

"I need to blow up something," she replied.

"I'll be at the dining room table when you're ready."

Jasmine hung up a few clothes and put some things away, then returned to the front of the building and sat down at the dining table.

Habib unrolled a map of the city. "There are a number of potential targets," he said, and they discussed each.

"I want the CIA station on the Upper East Side," she said.

Habib tapped his finger on the map. "It's right here. We've been surveilling it."

"Do they have an underground garage?"

"Yes, but it's well guarded." He showed her some photographs of the building. "There's a steel door with a keypad. Cars have to be admitted from the inside. The security station and barrier are about eight feet into the building," Habib said. "Covered by armed guards."

"Good," she said. "I like armed guards. Do you have a person to deliver?"

"I have two," Habib said. "A young man and a young woman."

"What sort of accent does the young man have?"

"American. He was born in Pakistan but came here at the age of two with his parents."

192

"The young man, then. I want him to drive a black Lincoln like the one that met me at the airport. It has a very large trunk, so we can maximize the size of the device. You have a reliable bomb builder?"

"I am the bomb builder," Habib replied, "and my devices are very reliable. I have one ready to go. I need only add more plastique to fill the trunk."

"I want cell phone activation," she said, "and I want to be here." She tapped a spot on the map around the corner from the garage entrance. "In a New York yellow taxi."

"I will drive you," he said. "I think it is best you do not try to make an escape by car. Immediately after the detonation, the streets will become impassable. There is a subway station here." He tapped the map. "You should take the subway twenty stops downtown, to here." He moved his finger downtown. "Another car will meet you there and bring you up the West Side to this house. I will supply you with a Metrocard."

"Excellent," she said.

"Why do you want to observe the attack?" he asked.

"Because it will give me pleasure," she replied. "Let's execute during rush hour tomorrow morning. Is that feasible?"

"Perfectly. We have only to obtain the two vehicles, which will be done tonight."

"Good. Now I will have some food and a nap."

Stone and Holly were sitting up in bed having a full English breakfast from a room-service cart. The TV was on the morning news, and the news was of heavy fog in London, preventing most flights.

"Looks like we might be stuck here another day," Holly said.

"I can handle that," Stone replied. "We can just keep ordering room service."

"Stone, you are always good in bed, but last night was really something."

"Takes two," Stone replied, biting into a muffin.

The phone rang, and Holly answered. "Yes?"

"It's Inspector Harry Tate," a male voice said.

"Good morning, Inspector."

"I thought you might like a report on the raincoat we took from your State Department's personnel office."

"Yes, indeed." She motioned to Stone to pick up the phone on his side, then put a finger to her lips.

"The coat was unremarkable — a cheap

knockoff of a Burberry raincoat, and we got nothing from the coat itself."

"Was there something else?"

"There was a lipstick in one pocket," Tate said. "The fingerprints were smudged, but we got enough DNA for a match. If we get her, we can place her at the office definitively."

"Very good, Inspector," Holly said. "Would you be kind enough to get the DNA profile to our FBI?"

"Of course, and to Langley, too."

"That's very kind of you."

"Is there anything else we can do for you?"

"A latitude and longitude on Jasmine Shazaz would be very nice."

"The moment we get it. Good morning." He hung up.

Stone and Holly hung up, too. "I suppose that's progress of a kind," he said.

"Yes," Holly replied. "Now we'll be able to positively identify her remains."

"That's pretty cold of you," Stone said.

"Yes, it is," Holly said. "I find myself getting colder about these things."

30

Jasmine sat in the rear of her stolen taxicab, leaning against a door and looking out the rear window toward the building on the corner behind her.

Habib's cell phone rang. "Yes? Thank you." He hung up and turned around. "The car is one minute out," he said.

"You gave the driver my instructions?"

"Yes. When he rings the bell he is to say that his passenger is Director Katharine Lee."

"Good. Now let's move down the street to the end of this block. I'll still be able to see the garage door from there, and I don't think we want to be this close."

"As you wish." Habib put the idling taxi into gear and rolled down the street. As he stopped, a young woman walked up to the cab and rapped on the front passenger window.

Jasmine stiffened. "What does she want?"

Habib rolled down the window and accepted a shopping bag from the young woman, then he rolled up the window, and she walked away. He turned around and handed Jasmine the shopping bag. "Cover," he said. "Purchases from Bloomingdale's made a few minutes ago, complete with receipts."

"Good," Jasmine said, breathing a sigh of relief. She looked out the rear window. "Here comes our package," she said.

The black Lincoln turned into the driveway of the corner building, blocking the sidewalk. She watched as the driver's window slid down and a hand reached out toward the metal box cantilevered toward arriving cars. Half a minute's wait ensued, then the garage door rolled up, and the Lincoln drove inside. Suddenly, flashes of light came from the garage, and she heard automatic weapons fire. She pressed the speed dial button on her cell phone. Seconds later, a roar of sound and flame erupted from the garage, engulfing pedestrians and cars on the street.

"Go," Jasmine said, but she did not stop looking out the window. "The building didn't collapse," she said.

"Perhaps it is strongly reinforced," Habib replied, putting the cab into gear and turning downtown at the next corner. "Subway coming up on your right," he said.

She handed him the cell phone. "Dispose of this," she said, then hipped her way across the backseat and got out of the cab, which immediately drove away. She saw the off-duty sign on top go on.

Jasmine walked down into the subway station, inserted her Metrocard in the slot, and made her way through the turnstile. She had stood on the platform for less than a minute when the train arrived, and a flood of people got off. She waited for them to clear the car, then got on and took a seat. She checked her pulse: seventy-two, not bad. She began taking slow, deep breaths, and she noticed that she felt wet between her legs. The train rolled out of the station; after it had traveled only a few yards the lights went out in the car and the train squealed to a halt. Probably a momentary power failure, she thought, but it turned out not to be momentary. She sat in the car for perhaps five minutes when she realized that the train had probably been deliberately stopped.

A uniformed policeman entered the car from ahead. "Stay in your seats, please. This is a police stop. We'll get moving again as soon as we can."

The train had stopped for her, she realized. She opened her bag and removed the wallet Habib had given her the night before, containing a New York ID and several hundred dollars in cash. For just a moment, she considered trying to get the car door open and fleeing down the tunnel, but she restrained herself.

They sat there quietly in the dark for another seven or eight minutes, then the lights came back on, but the train still did not move. She looked out the window and saw flashlights playing on the wall of the tunnel, and a moment later the door to the car behind her opened, and four men, two of them uniformed policemen, came into her car.

"Listen up, everybody." He held up a badge. "We are New York City police officers, and we are going to check the ID of everybody on this car," he said. "Now sit quietly and keep your hands where we can see them. Get out your ID and be prepared to show it."

Jasmine took the wallet from her large purse and removed the New York State driver's license from it. The cops worked their way down the car, checking IDs, and finally stopped in front of her.

A detective took the driver's license from

her hand and compared the photo on it with her face. "What's your address?" he asked.

"Five-ninety Park Avenue," she said, reciting the address on the license.

"Where did you get on the train?"

"At the last station."

"Where were you before that?"

"At Bloomingdale's," she said, holding up her shopping bag.

He dipped into it and came up with a cashmere scarf and some panty hose. "Handbag?" he said.

She opened her handbag and held it up to him. He rummaged in it for a moment. Then stepped away. "Thank you for your cooperation," he said, then moved on to the next passenger.

Another half an hour passed before the train began to move again. Jasmine picked up a discarded *New York Post* from the seat beside her and began to read it. She was safe.

She got off at the specified stop and looked around. A young man lounging against a Toyota sedan stood up straight and looked at her. She walked toward him.

"Ms. Avery?" he asked.

"Yes," she replied.

He held open the car door for her, and

she got in.

He turned right at the next corner. "We're going over to the West Side Highway," he said. The East Side is all screwed up with traffic."

"I understand," she replied.

The driver made his way across town slowly. "The traffic is always like this," he said. "Nothing unusual."

"Fine."

Twenty minutes later, he drove past the safe house slowly, and they both looked for signs of police. He let her off at the next corner and she walked back to the house, careful not to hurry. She went to the basement door and rang the bell.

The door opened almost immediately, and Habib let her in. "Everything all right?"

"Perfectly normal. There was one surprise: they stopped the subway train. It must be part of their plan after an attack."

"That's new to us."

"The Bloomingdale's bag was a brilliant idea. It may have saved me from further interrogation."

"Thank you. I believe we're safe in this house, no need to move you again."

"I'll take a day or two off before we begin again," she said.

31

Holly was awakened by the flight attendant, who was holding a tray. "Some lunch?"

"Thank you," Holly replied. Stone was already eating his.

"We've had several satphone calls," the attendant said, "but nobody on the line. It may be some equipment or satellite problem. You might check in as soon as we land."

"Thank you," Holly said, and began to eat her sandwich.

As the Gulfstream touched down, Holly switched on her cell phone: there were three voice messages and a text, all telling her to call the director's office. The airplane taxied to a halt, and Holly and Stone deplaned and got into the waiting car. While they waited for their luggage to be loaded, Holly called in on the director's direct line. A moment later she was connected.

"Hello, Holly, we've been trying to reach you."

"The satphone on the airplane wasn't working," Holly said. "I called back as soon as I could. I'm at Teterboro now."

"Bad news. We've had a bombing at the East Side station."

Holly gulped. "How bad?"

"Two security people killed, plus the driver of the Lincoln Town Car containing the bomb. He used my name to get the garage door opened. Three people in the street, on foot or in cars, were killed, too, and some damage was done to the front wall of a town house across the street. The New York media are all over us, but our cover story is still holding. We're saying that the building contained some administrative people."

"What was the damage to our building?"

"The reinforced garage contained it. Lots of vehicle damage, but that has already been cleared away, and the garage is operating normally again."

"Any suspects?"

"Al Qaeda, of course."

"Jasmine?"

"You think she's in the country?"

"I think it's likely," Holly replied.

"The FBI has circulated her photograph,

but only a few hours ago. She could have entered the country before that happened."

"I think you should take greater than usual personal precautions," Holly said. "Helicopter to and from work. Remember the British foreign minister."

"I have new security arrangements in hand," Kate replied, "and so does the secretary of state. I want you to stay in New York and make sure everything in the building is running normally and that additional security arrangements have been made before you come back here."

"Yes, ma'am," Holly replied.

"You'll be staying at Stone's house?"

"I'll be reachable on my cell."

"Don't be coy. I want you protected."

"Yes, ma'am, I'll be staying at Stone's." She raised her eyebrows questioningly, and he nodded.

"We'll speak after you've assessed the situation on the East Side," Kate said.

Holly hung up. "Jasmine's here," she said to Stone.

"In the city?"

Holly nodded. "There was a bombing at our New York station. We'll drop you, then I'll go directly there. Thank you for continuing to put me up."

"I'm glad to have you."

204

"Expect security outside your house."

"I'm glad to have that, too."

Holly sat back in her seat and sighed. "I think I'm glad Jasmine is here," she said.

"Why?"

"Because I couldn't do anything about catching her in London. Here, it's going to be different."

The garage door was operating when her car arrived at the station, but an armed guard looked into the car before the door was opened. Inside, a new security barrier was being installed, and the garage was nearly empty of cars.

Upstairs, Holly took her usual office, then called the station chief. "I want a meeting with the FBI AIC and the police commissioner as soon as possible," she said.

"Where?"

"Let them decide. How are we fixed for armored vehicles?"

"There were two in the garage — one burned, the other is being repaired. Should be back within the hour."

"I'll use that to go to the meeting," she said. "Have them pick me up here." She gave him Stone's address. "And I want security outside that address, starting now.

I'm staying there. How's everybody holding up here?"

"They're all being very cool about it," he replied.

"Good. Let's keep it as normal as possible."

"Will do."

"How did the bomber car get into the garage?"

"The driver told us that Director Lee was in the car," he said. "Almost as soon as the door was opened, shots were fired, so the guards knew immediately that the car was a threat. Then the bomb went off. We think the driver was already dead when it blew."

"Anything on the driver?"

"He's hamburger. The feds took the pieces for examination. The bomb was in the trunk, so much of the force of the blast went into the street. The rest just hit cars."

"Traffic was normal when I arrived."

"It took the police a couple of hours to clear the block, then they reopened it."

"What's happening with the media?"

"We've referred all inquiries to the police commissioner's office, and they're stating that we're just federal office workers. That story seems to be holding, for the moment."

"Good."

Two hours later Holly sat in the police commissioner's office with the commissioner and the agent in charge of the FBI's New York office.

"The car and the body of the driver have yielded little," the AIC said, "except that he is of Middle Eastern descent. His prints weren't on file."

Holly nodded.

"We've got everybody on this," the commissioner said.

"It's Jasmine Shazaz," Holly said.

"How do you know that?" the AIC asked.

"I can't prove it, but I know it."

"That's not how we work."

"You got the photograph yesterday," Holly said. "When did personnel at entry points have it?"

The AIC looked at his fingernails. "It takes time," he said. "It's there now."

"She probably entered the country during the past twenty-four hours," Holly said.

"How could she plan a thing so quickly?" the commissioner asked.

"I should think it was already planned by a team here. She probably selected it from a menu of targets. They've already wreaked havoc in London. Be prepared for it to happen here."

"We're doing everything we can," the commissioner said.

"I hope it's enough," Holly replied.

32

Jasmine had another nap, then came to dinner. Habib had ordered in. He held her chair; the food was Indian.

"Wine?" she asked.

"I'm Muslim, aren't you?"

"Not your kind of Muslim," she replied. "Send somebody out for it — a nice California Chardonnay will do."

Habib gave the order, and the wine was back in ten minutes. "May we dine now?" he asked.

"Of course." Jasmine opened the bottle, so Habib wouldn't be sullied, and poured herself a large glass, then she helped herself to the food. "It's good," she said.

"I think you should leave New York," Habib said. "There will be a very great search for you."

"Certainly not. I have work to do here. Let's have another look at your list."

Habib got up and brought the list.

Jasmine took a sip of her wine and consulted the paper. "These buildings are too secure. We got lucky at the CIA place."

"They'll be expecting you to bomb those sorts of places," he said.

"I want something different, but something that still hurts. Let's go back to the CIA building."

"We can't do that," Habib said.

"We can do whatever we wish," Jasmine replied, trying not to sound too sharp. Habib was not accustomed to being bossed around by women, after all. "Send someone to the neighborhood, someone who won't be noticed. Have him watch the people who leave at lunchtime."

"All right. We've had a report that the woman from the CIA sent to London after the attack at the embassy has left London and returned to New York."

"How do we know this?"

"A spotter at London City Airport recorded the landing from the States of a Gulfstream 450 jet which we have seen deliver CIA personnel in the past. The following morning a man and a woman boarded that aircraft, which flew to Teterboro, New Jersey, according to the flight plan filed." Habib put a photograph of the two on the table. "She was seen leaving the

Connaught Hotel an hour before it took off. We believe she boarded the airplane. The name on the manifest was H. Barker, and there's a Holly Barker high up at the CIA."

"So you had plenty of time to place someone at Teterboro, didn't you?"

"Teterboro is a different basket of fish than London City. It's the largest and busiest general aviation airport in the United States, and it has half a dozen places — they call them FBOs — where the airplane could park. We confirmed that the airplane landed, but our observer was off the field and had to guess where it parked from the direction it taxied."

"And?"

"He went to Jet Aviation and through the fence saw a black SUV, such as the CIA uses, be allowed onto the ramp, which is unusual. Suspecting it was a government vehicle, he followed it into the city, where it made a stop in the East Forties, letting a man out, then continued. Unfortunately, our man lost contact with the car when it continued, but it was not so far from the CIA building."

"This place in the East Forties — what was it?"

"A town house, in a neighborhood called Turtle Bay."

"Who lives there?"

"We think the man who flew with Barker, but we're not sure."

"Have the house watched," she said, "along with the CIA building."

"It will be done."

"I want to know what connection the woman from the CIA has with the man who lives there."

Habib nodded.

"How many bombs do we have available?"

"One, assembled. We can obtain materials for as many as we need."

"Assemble a second bomb," Jasmine said.

Stone and Holly sat at a corner table at Patroon, Stone's new favorite restaurant. He missed the clublike atmosphere and the regulars at Elaine's, but the food was good here and the atmosphere warm and inviting.

"How bad was it?" Stone asked.

"Not nearly as bad as it might have been," Holly said. "We built the building, and we built it to survive an explosion virtually intact."

"Is it Jasmine?"

"Of course it is. I had a meeting with the police commissioner and the AIC from the FBI's local office, and I explained about her, but I'm not sure they bought it. The FBI was slow to circulate her photo, and she made it into the country. That drives me crazy!"

"Does Jasmine know who you are?"

"I have no reason to think so," Holly replied. "She knows who the director is, though, and I've warned her to stop driving to work and take the helicopter instead."

"Sounds like good advice."

"It's all I can do. We're no better equipped for a hunt in New York than we were in London, and we don't have any more authority, either. Sometimes I think we need a change in our charter. I think we would have been a better place to spend the taxpayers' money than creating this gargantuan Homeland Security apparatus."

"Have you talked with them?"

"I'm relying on the FBI to do that," she said. "I have to keep the peace."

"I haven't heard anything on the news about a search for Jasmine," Stone said.

"I know, and it's frustrating."

"Do you think she's still here?"

"I have no way of knowing. She could be anywhere in the country by now."

"Maybe Kate Lee needs to go to the president about this."

"She'll know better than I when it's time

to do that."

"I suppose so."

Holly finished her glass of wine and waited for Stone to refill her glass, then she took a healthy swig of that.

"I saw two men in a car near my house," Stone said. "Are they yours?"

"They'd better be," Holly said.

"Why don't you invite them into the house? Put one inside my office outside door and one in the kitchen — that way they can watch both the street and the garden."

"You don't mind?"

"Mind? I don't want my house blown up."

"I'll do it, then."

"I feel better already," Stone said.

33

Joan buzzed Stone. "Herbie on one."

Stone pressed the button. "Morning, Herb. How are you?"

"Extremely well," Herbie replied. "And you?"

"Can't complain." He didn't mention that there was CIA security at the front and rear of his house.

"Is Holly in town?"

"She is."

"Will the two of you have dinner with Harp and me this evening?"

"Let me check with Holly — hang on." Stone pressed the hold button, rang Holly and got an affirmative reply.

"Sure, where and when?"

"La Grenouille at eight?"

"Nice choice. We'll be there." They both hung up. Stone reflected that he was unable to keep up with Herbie's progress as a sophisticate. A year before he would never

215

have heard of La Grenouille.

Stone and Holly arrived at the restaurant a little late, and Stone was surprised to find James Rutledge and Kelli Keane at the table with Herbie and Harp. He introduced Holly, and they sat down.

A waiter appeared with a bottle of Veuve Clicquot Grande Dame champagne and presented it to Herbie, who nodded. "Would anyone prefer something else to drink? Stone, I'm sure they have Knob Creek."

"My favorite champagne is always good enough for me," Stone said, as the waiter made his rounds, then brought them menus.

"When is your book out, Kelli?" Stone asked.

"Very soon," she replied.

"I hope I'm not going to get a raft of calls from the media."

"I think all their questions will be answered in the book," she said, cryptically.

"It's too late for 'no comment,' then?"

"I don't think you have anything to worry about, Stone." She turned to Holly. "I remember you from the opening of The Arrington in L.A. You're CIA, aren't you?" Asked as if they had never met.

"That's right."

"Congratulations on your promotion,"

Kelli said. "I saw the mention in the *Times.*"

"Thank you," Holly replied.

"I believe you had some sort of bombing incident on the East Side, didn't you?"

"Yes."

"Any significant damage?"

"It rattled a few coffee cups — that was about it."

"I'll bet that's what you would say if the building were just a hole in the ground," Kelli said, laughing.

"Probably."

"Have you been with the Agency a long time?"

"A fairly long time."

"Did you do something else before that?"

"I was a police officer in Florida. Before that I was in the army, where I was a police officer, too."

"I didn't know the Agency drew on former police as recruits."

"The Agency recruits from all over the place," Holly replied. She was being careful; she didn't often have conversations about her work with civilians, and this woman was a journalist and the subject of an investigation she herself had initiated.

"Do you enjoy the work?"

"It's very gratifying, when things go well. When they don't, less so."

"How did you and Stone meet?"

"We first met when I was still working in Florida. Some years ago."

"Are you staying with Stone while you're here?"

"I have an apartment in the city," Holly replied, offering half a lie. "How about you? Do you and Jim live together?"

Kelli didn't blink. "Yes, we do."

"Uptown or down?"

"Downtown. Jim has a loft, and I'm lucky having a man who is a brilliant designer. You must come down for dinner one night soon."

"That would be very nice," Holly said, though she had a very, very good idea what the apartment looked like.

"I hear today from an acquaintance at the FBI that they're looking for a woman in connection with the bombing."

"That's perfectly true," Holly said.

"Who is she?"

Now Holly had to decide whether to toss a grenade into the conversation. It didn't take her long. "Her name is Jasmine Shazaz. Does that ring a bell?"

"No, it doesn't."

"She is the sister of a man named Ari Shazaz. How about that name?"

"No, I've never heard it."

"Perhaps you knew him as McCallister. He was in L.A., too."

That stopped Kelli in her tracks. "Ah, yes," she managed to say.

"He and his brother were killed while trying to escape the country after the L.A. incident."

"So Jasmine is out for revenge?"

"That appears to be the case. She has been connected to two recent bombings in London — one that killed the British foreign minister, the other at the American Embassy."

"Of course, I knew about that," Kelli said.

"But you didn't know the backstory?"

"No, I didn't. May I write about this?"

"Yes, if you refer to me as a confidential source."

"Are there other people I can talk to?"

"You can try the police commissioner and the head of the New York office of the FBI, but I don't know how much they'll have to say."

"Why haven't I seen anything about Jasmine Shazaz in the papers or on TV?"

"That would be a good question for the commissioner and the FBI," Holly replied, "but don't tell them you talked to me."

"I'm a magazine writer, not a daily journalist," Kelli said. "I'd need a lot more than this to get a piece into, say, *Vanity Fair.*"

"I'm afraid there isn't a lot more I can tell you. You can also try the British Foreign Office and New Scotland Yard's Special Branch."

"They're not going to tell me much either, are they?" Kelli asked.

"Perhaps not. Perhaps you should hold your piece until there is a successful conclusion to the case. I'm sure a lot of people would be more interested in talking at that time."

"Would you be?"

"I'm afraid not. I'm sure you know that we don't operate domestically."

The waiter returned, and they placed their orders. Kelli did not return to the subject of Jasmine.

34

Back at Stone's house Holly took her laptop into her dressing room, logged onto the Agency mainframe, and accessed the surveillance at James Rutledge's apartment. She got the two just as they came through the front door.

"Well, that was fun," Jim was saying. "You seemed to enjoy Holly Barker's company."

"It wasn't the first time we met," Kelli replied, hanging her coat in the hall closet.

"That's right, you met in L.A."

"Only in passing."

"You've met her since?"

"Yes. She and I had a rather scary conversation."

"About what?"

They moved into the bedroom, but Holly still caught the audio.

"About something she doesn't want me to talk about."

"We're back to that, are we? You know

something I don't know. All right, if you don't want to tell me, don't, but please stop bringing it up."

"I didn't bring it up, you did," she said, unzipping her dress and stepping out of it.

"No, you . . . Oh, never mind."

They got undressed in silence and got into bed. There was enough light in the room for the high-definition cameras to register their images. Jim made a move for a breast, kissing her on a nipple. Kelli responded, and soon they were at it.

Holly used the interval to get undressed herself, then she went back to the computer. The two were lying in bed, breathing hard, spent.

"All right, I'll tell you," Kelli said. She rolled over and put her lips close to his ear.

This Holly couldn't hear.

"You're shitting me," Jim said.

"I shit you not."

"Christ, no wonder the CIA doesn't want that out. Do you think the cameras we had taken out were put there by the Agency?"

"I did at first, but now I think it might be somebody at a rival publication, a tabloid called *The Instigator.* They've done this before — tapped phones, et cetera."

"Why would they try to listen in on us?"

"Because they're out to subvert *Vanity Fair,*

and they desperately want to know what the magazine is going to publish. They have a shorter lead time, and if they find out what other writers and I are writing for *VF,* they can get something in their rag first."

"Do you think they tried to run you down, too?"

"No, I'm beginning to think that was just an accident."

"You mean, you're admitting I'm right?" he asked, laughing.

"Don't let it go to your head, buster," Kelli said.

They got quiet, and Holly switched off her computer and went into the bedroom, naked as usual.

"What were you doing in there for so long?" Stone asked.

"Girl stuff," Holly replied, climbing into bed. "You want to talk, or you want to fuck?"

Stone switched off the light.

Later, when they were lying in each other's arms, half asleep, Stone said, "You and Kelli Keane were kind of into it tonight. What was that about?"

"Like any good journalist, she was pumping me for information about the explosion at our station."

"Did you tell her anything?"

"Actually, I did — just enough to get her calling the police commissioner and the FBI. Maybe that will get their asses in gear."

"Getting their asses in gear would be a major achievement," Stone said.

"Tell me about it. This job is more fun when I don't have to deal with people outside the Agency. I haven't really learned yet how to push the buttons of people like the commissioner and the AIC at the Bureau."

"Sounds like you're doing pretty well, getting Kelli in on the action. She can be a bulldog."

"Are you worried about her book coming out?"

"I'm a little anxious," Stone admitted. "Not because there'll be anything terrible in it, but because a lot of people will read it, and I'll get a lot of calls, and so will Peter. It will probably haunt me for years to come."

"Are you worried about what Peter will think?"

"Not so much. There's a lot he doesn't know, and some of it will be in Kelli's book, saving me from having to tell him about it."

"I'm lucky I didn't have kids," Holly said. "I'd be in the position of having them ask about what I do all the time."

"And eventually, they'd find out."

"Maybe more than I'd want them to know."

Holly slipped into sleep on Stone's shoulder, and Stone followed shortly.

35

Holly was working at her desk when a security guard rapped on her door. "You ordered a sandwich delivery?" He held up a paper bag.

"Yes, thanks. What do I owe you?"

He looked at the receipt stapled to the bag. "Twelve-fifty. I gave him fifteen."

Holly got the money from her handbag and handed it to him. "Thanks for not making me look like a cheapskate."

He waved and went back to his post in the downstairs lobby, where he was one of four these days, two of them posing as people waiting to see people upstairs.

Holly unwrapped the sandwich and set it on her desk, then opened the can of diet soda that had come with it. She was extremely hungry and was about to bite into it when she heard a muffled explosion from the direction of the avenue. The reinforced walls and armored triple glazing in her building kept out nearly all noise; something she could hear at all would have to be big.

Holly went to the window and looked outside. Down the block a few doors and at street level she could see the facade of a building blown away and twisted cars in the street, lying in disarray. A few people were picking themselves up from the rubble, and they were all bloody.

Holly picked up the phone and pressed the paging button. "Security, this is Assistant Director Barker: call nine-one-one, ask for every available policeman and ambulance. Everybody who's armed, on the street, but stay away from the site of the explosion. Whoever did this is in a car or a cab nearby. Look for a woman in the rear seat. Compare to the flyer on the downstairs reception desk. Move!"

She slung her bag on her shoulder and ran down the hallway, skipped the elevator, and ran down the stairs. The four security men in the reception room were looking out the small window in the door. "One of you man the phones, the rest of you follow me!" she yelled at them. She stuck her hand in her bag, held her hand on her pistol, and stepped into the street, looking both ways. "You and you," she yelled to two of them, "go down the block that way. You," she said to the other one, "follow me."

Holly ran up the block in the street, her hand still in her bag, looking into every vehicle as she went. At the next corner she looked both ways, then ran across the street and into a subway station, waving for her man to follow her.

She leaped the stile and headed down the escalator, holding one position and looking at every person ahead of her.

There, she thought, standing on the platform, back to her, waiting for the train.

"That one," she said to her man, pointing. "Approach with caution, but fast. Police!" she yelled, parting the people ahead of her on the escalator and pushing past them, the gun out now. As she hit the bottom, she flicked off the safety with her thumb; one round already in the chamber. Her man moved up beside her. The train came rumbling into the station, the air brakes hissing as it stopped. The crowd on the platform surged forward onto the car, blocking her way.

She was nearly to the car when the doors closed. Swearing under her breath, she ran alongside the car as it began to move. A woman sat down on the other side of the car, facing her. Jasmine. Holly brought up the weapon, but a wall was coming at her as the train went into the tunnel, and she had to stop.

She dug into her bag and came up with her cell phone, pressed a button.

"NYPD. Commissioner's office," a male voice said.

"Emergency! This is Assistant Director Holly Barker of the CIA. Give me the commissioner now!"

The commissioner came on the line five seconds later. "Holly?"

"Explosion across the street from our building — a restaurant, I think. I've already called it in. One of my men and I pursued Jasmine into a subway station on Lex. She's headed downtown. Have them stop the trains."

"It's already being done — part of our protocol."

The lights went off in the station, and Holly heard brakes hissing from down the tunnel. "Have them detain every unaccompanied woman who comes close to Jasmine's description," she said, then broke the connection and dug into her bag for the small but powerful lithium-powered flashlight she carried everywhere. She turned to the man behind her. "Come on!" She turned on the flashlight, jumped onto the tracks, and started running, the man close on her heels.

"What's your name?" she shouted back at him.

"Troy."

"You've seen the flyer with the woman's photograph?"

"Yes, ma'am."

"We're going into the last car on the train and work our way forward. She will resist, and she may have an explosive or a gun. Take no chances, be prepared to kill her."

"I'm with you!"

Holly could see the train fifty yards ahead, now. The emergency lighting had come on in the cars, and they were dimly lit. She reached the rear car, got a foot on a step, and grabbed the door handle. Locked. She banged on the glass with the butt of her gun, and someone looked at her from inside. A man came and opened the door.

"Police!" she yelled. "Stand back!" Her man climbed in behind her, and she started moving down the packed car, the flashlight playing on each face. Nothing in the first car. She moved into the next car and searched it thoroughly, then moved on to another car. This one was very crowded, and as she opened the door, she saw a side door open ahead of her. "Police!" she kept yelling. "Everybody down!" People hit the floor in a hurry, and she could see the open door. She leaped over the prostrate people and jumped out the door, looking both ways.

Troy jumped down beside her. "I saw somebody run past the car on the tracks, headed back uptown. I couldn't tell if it was a woman."

"That way, then!" Holly yelled, and started to run back the way she had come. She checked between each car as she passed, then shone her small beam down the tracks. A shape was moving away from her. She ran after it.

Ahead another sixty yards or so she saw someone trying to climb onto the platform, and a couple of men were helping her. Holly sprinted toward the spot. "Troy!" she yelled. "Give me a leg up!" He did and she hit the platform on her knees and got to her feet. "Police!" she yelled at the crowd. "Which way did she go?"

Half a dozen people pointed toward the escalator. "Come on, Troy, the power is off. We'll gain on her!" She elbowed her way through the crowd, shouting at them to get out of her way, and as she did, the station lights came on.

"Shit!" she yelled, and kept on, making

her way toward the escalator, now operating. She ran up the moving steps, yelling at people, moving as fast as she could in the crowd. The station level was only a few yards ahead. She broke free of the crowd at the top of the escalator and ran toward the exit. She couldn't see anyone who looked like Jasmine.

She got through the exit stile and ran toward the street, the daylight welcoming her. Then she was on the sidewalk, looking both ways. Traffic was at a halt. She leaped onto the hood of a taxi and climbed on top, giving her a good view in both directions.

Troy joined her, saying nothing, just looking.

"Anything?" Holly asked.

"Nothing," Troy replied.

Holly let out a lungful of air. "That's what I see, too," she said.

The cabdriver got out of his cab. "Hey!" he yelled. "What the fuck are you doing?"

"Tap dancing on your roof," Holly replied.

36

Holly went through the building, checking who was out. "A lot of us had lunch at that place two or three times a week," a secretary told her. Holly made a list of names of people not in the building. Finally, she went down and called the director.

"Holly, I've been waiting for your call. I was told you were in pursuit."

"I was, with a security guard named Troy, and we came close. She was on the subway, but she made it back onto the tracks and to the station while we were dealing with knots of passengers. She disappeared on Lexington Avenue."

"Casualties?"

"Don't know yet," Holly replied. "Fourteen people are not in the office, plus one who called in sick. The restaurant that was bombed was popular with our people, so we're looking at losses. I haven't heard the news reports, but I don't see how anybody

233

inside the place could survive that explosion. We're going to have to keep everybody in the building for their whole shifts until we get Jasmine and her bunch."

"Issue that order soonest," Kate replied. "Call me back when you have a body count. I want names."

"Yes, ma'am." Holly hung up, wrung out from her massive expenditure of adrenaline. She closed the door and locked it, then flopped onto the sofa and was quickly asleep.

She was awakened later by someone hammering on her door, and she struggled to her feet and opened it. A woman she recognized as an analyst was standing there, holding a sheet of paper.

"What time is it?" Holly asked.

"Five minutes to four," the woman replied, handing her the sheet. "This is a list of everybody who didn't come back from lunch."

"Sorry, I was out," Holly said, taking the list.

"I understand."

Holly looked at the list. "They should all be back?"

"Yes. We've got one out sick, the rest are all accounted for."

"Spread the word: nobody goes out for lunch during a shift. If the food in the cafeteria isn't good enough, I'll do something about it."

"I'll do that," the woman said, "and we could use a proper chef, instead of the dietitian. People say the food is a cross between prison and school dining hall."

"Come on in," Holly said. She sat down at her computer and typed for a moment, then sent it to the printer and got a couple of dozen copies. "Hand these around, and put one on every bulletin board," she said. "I'll do something about the food."

The woman took the memo and left. Holly called the director.

"Yes, Holly?"

"Looks like six of our people died — three secretaries, two analysts, and a computer tech. I'll e-mail you the names, but I don't think you should release them to anyone, including families, until we have identity confirmation from the coroner's office."

"All right. Is there anything I can do?"

"Yes, ma'am. Authorize the hiring of a chef. Everybody hates the food in the cafeteria."

There was a short pause. "I remember," she said. "I'll put somebody from our design department on turning the place into a proper restaurant, and I'll tell personnel to find a chef. I've got some discretionary budget I haven't used."

"That's a wonderful idea," Holly said. "Now I won't have to bring a lunch box."

"I'm afraid you're stuck there until this is resolved," Kate said.

"I'm happy to deal with it, Director. May I make a suggestion?"

"Of course."

"It would be great if the president, since he's leaving office, would see about authorizing us to work domestically in terrorism cases."

"Funny you should mention that. We talked about it a couple of days ago, and last night Will told me that he's sending a request to the Senate Select Committee on Intelligence to get a bill together to authorize. The White House counsel has told him he can issue an executive order to permit us to work domestically, but that it will expire with his presidency. I've asked him to make his request to the committee on an emergency basis, and what has happened today will make it imperative that they move quickly. He'll sign the executive order today."

"Thank you, ma'am," Holly said, and she meant it. "May I tell our people here? It might help morale. Everybody knew somebody who was in that restaurant."

"Go ahead and tell them, but warn them that the information is classified until they read it in the papers."

"Yes, ma'am. May I tell the police commissioner and the FBI AIC?"

"Yes." The director hung up. Holly called the police commissioner.

"Yes, Holly. Don't worry, we're all over this."

Holly told him about the chase in the subway tunnel.

"I'm sorry you weren't able to shoot her," he said. "That's twice she's eluded capture."

"Thank you, sir. I need your help on two things."

"Anything."

"First, I need confirmation from the morgue, soonest, of the ID of our people who were in the restaurant. Our best guess is six, and I'll e-mail you the names."

"Of course. I'll call the ME myself."

"The other thing is, the president is signing an executive order today to give the Agency the right to work domestically on terrorism cases. This will be the first one."

"Can he do that?"

"Yes, but the order will expire with his presidency. He's making an emergency request to the Intelligence Committee in the Senate for legislation modifying our charter to that effect."

"You won't hear any complaints from me about that," the commissioner replied. "We can use all the help we can get. I can't speak for the FBI."

"I'll ask the director to ask the president to call their director. Maybe they'll take it better if the news comes down from the top."

"Good idea. I don't want to have to listen to their pissing and moaning."

"One more thing, Commissioner: you've got to go public with the photograph of Jasmine Shazaz."

"I agree," he replied. "I'll give the order to Public Affairs immediately, and the FBI can lump it."

"Thank you, sir." She hung up. Her computer chimed, signaling a priority e-mail, and she logged on. "This is going out to everybody in the New York office," Kate wrote. "From now on, it's the New York station."

Holly read the following bulletin. "To the staff in New York: I know you've all lost friends today, and our hearts are with you. As the result of their sacrifice, the president of the United States has today signed an executive order allowing the Agency to operate domestically in terrorism cases, and he has requested that the Congress, on an emergency basis, authorize a change to our charter to that effect.

"Accordingly, the New York office is now the New York station, and Assistant Director Holly Barker is appointed station chief. I know you will all give her the help she needs.

"Finally, since I've ordered that no one leave the building for lunch, I have directed that a chef be hired and that the cafeteria be remodeled into a proper restaurant. I've asked that it be up and running in a week. In the meantime, bring good things to eat to work." Signed, Katharine Rule, Director.

"Station chief," Holly said aloud to herself. "I don't believe it."

37

Holly left the office at eight o'clock, to meet Stone at P. J. Clarke's. By the time she got there the usual crowd at the bar had subsided, and Stone was leaning against it with a drink in his hand. He signaled the bartender for one more.

"I saw everything on New York One," he said, referring to the local cable news channel. "I'm sorry about the loss of your people."

Holly took a deep draft of her drink. "It's the worst working day of my life," she said. "I knew a couple of them, though not well. Tomorrow I have to write letters to their families, and I'm not looking forward to that."

"It's Jasmine?"

Holly nodded. "I damn near had her in my sights this afternoon, but she got away."

"That's rough. I hope you get her next time."

Holly tossed off her drink and set down the empty glass. "I missed lunch. Can we sit down?"

"Sure." Stone put money on the bar and led her to the back room, where a table was waiting. They ordered steaks immediately.

"Stone, a couple of other things happened today," she said.

"I heard on the news about the president's executive order."

"And as a result, the office here has been made a full-fledged station, and I'm the new station chief."

"So you'll be staying on in New York?"

"For the time being, until we're back on our feet and Jasmine has been dealt with. I think I should move to my apartment. I mean, it's just sitting there, I might as well get some use out of it."

"Have you taken a vow of celibacy?"

She squeezed his thigh. "Not yet!"

"Listen to me carefully: I suspect you're talking this way because you're afraid you're imposing on my good nature."

"Well . . ."

"Nothing could be further from the truth. I haven't felt so comfortable in my own house since Arrington died, and having you there has made me feel that way. Please stay with me for as long as you can stand it."

Holly smiled. "Standing it is not the problem. I'll stay."

"Good."

"I'll need to go up to my apartment and get some clothes, though."

"Plenty of room in your dressing room in Turtle Bay."

"Thank you, Stone."

"It'll save the Agency money on security, too. They'll have only one residence to guard."

"I suppose that's true. Do you mind if I admit to Kate Rule that I'm living with you? She assumes it anyway."

"Go right ahead. We can take out an ad in the paper, if you like."

"I don't think it's a good idea to advertise," Holly said, laughing.

"Right. Jasmine might see the ad, and we don't want that. May I make a suggestion?"

"Sure."

"Why don't you get an Agency driver and use my car to go to and from work every day?"

"Oh, thank you, but we have armored vehicles and drivers available at the station. I guess I'd better start using them, instead of taking cabs."

"Please do," Stone said. "I'd feel better."

Their food came and they dug in. When

they were on their last glass of wine, Holly cleared her throat. "I need your advice," she said.

"Of course. Legal?"

"In a way. I'm trying to figure out a way not to commit murder."

"I hope I can help. Who's the putative victim?"

"Kelli Keane."

"Oh?"

"She's told Jim Rutledge about the device at The Arrington."

Stone put down his glass. "How do you know that?"

"Because I had Rutledge's apartment wired for audio and video."

"And you've been listening in and watching?"

"From time to time. Last night I caught them coming back from our dinner and he was pumping her a little bit."

"Literally or figuratively?"

"Well, both, now that you mention it. They seem to do almost as much of that as you and I."

"Lucky them."

"But this time he was pumping her about an earlier conversation. She had told him she knew something that she couldn't tell him."

"And last night she told him everything?"

"She told him something, whispered in his ear, and from his reaction, I think she may have told him everything."

"And you're thinking about having her . . . What's the phrase they use in spy novels? Terminated with extreme prejudice?"

"That's the term. I'm not really going to do that, of course. My problem is, what do I do?"

"I believe you've already had a serious conversation with her about this, haven't you?"

"I have, and I thought I had scared her into silence. But . . ."

"But, she whispered into Jim's ear last night."

"Exactly. How can I shut her up?"

"Well, you could have them slapped around a little, I guess."

"Stop it! You're no help at all."

"All right, all right. Being an attorney, I tend to look for legal solutions to problems. I seem to recall reading about there being some federal judge that can secretly issue wiretap warrants for the FBI. Is that true?"

"I've heard that, too."

"Well, since the president has unleashed the Agency on an unsuspecting population with his executive order, wouldn't that give you access to the judge?"

"Very possibly," she said. "Go on."

"Well, you could formally request a gag order from the judge, barring Jim and Kelli from discussing the, ah, event with others. If they violated the order, they could be held in contempt of court and jailed indefinitely."

"What an attractive idea," Holly said, grinning. "I knew you'd come up with something."

Stone sighed. "There's another way to deal with the problem of leaks, though — a more honest way."

"What's that?"

"Get the president to reveal to the public what happened in L.A."

"Holy shit!" Holly exclaimed. "The media would go absolutely nuts!"

"Not as nuts as if they found out about it from Kelli or someone else who was there. It just may not be possible to keep a lid on this forever, and I think it would be better for the president, and for the country, if he were the one to tell them about it, instead of *The New York Times* or *Vanity Fair*. And you have the ear of the president, through Kate."

"I knew you'd tell me what to do," Holly said. "And I knew I wouldn't like doing it."

Stone shrugged. "An attorney gives advice

245

— hopefully good advice. It's not always fun to follow it."

38

They were back at Stone's house, having a nightcap in his study when Holly's cell phone went off. She looked at it. "It's the director," she said, "and at eleven o'clock at night. This can't be good." She pressed the button. "Good evening, Director."

"Holly, I have Felicity Devonshire on the line, and I want to conference you in, so that you can hear what she has to say directly from her. And I don't mind if Stone listens, too."

"Thank you, Director."

There was a click. "Holly?" Felicity asked. "Are you there?"

"Yes, Felicity." She thought about adding, "Stone, too," just to rub it in, but didn't.

"I'm sorry to call you so late."

"It's not as late as it is there," Holly said.

"Yes, well, we've been up all night. We've had a big break in the hunt for Jasmine."

"Go ahead."

"Early yesterday morning we got a tip from a milkman about a house on the Thames, west of London, quite a spiffy neighborhood. He said that he's seen Jasmine there twice in the past two weeks, and after a thorough interview with him we decided that the lead was good enough for a raid. And that's how we captured Habib Assam."

"I know that name — he's al Qaeda, isn't he?"

"He is — very important. We've had his brother in custody in the UK for nearly a year, and we made a lot of progress in turning him, but he wouldn't give up Habib. Now that he's in custody, the brother is talking."

"Wonderful. Has he given you anything on Jasmine?"

"Jasmine is part of his cell, as is Habib. He's telling us that there's a New York cell, too."

"How big a cell?"

"Half a dozen people, now plus Jasmine, working from an apartment somewhere on the West Side."

"Do you have an address?"

"I don't think he knows that, but there's more," Felicity said.

Holly didn't like the sound of that.

"There are cells in Boston, Chicago, Los Angeles, and Atlanta, too, each with something on the order of four to six people. The brother says they are all well supplied with weapons and explosives and ready to move when they get the order."

"From whom?" Holly asked.

"Ayman al-Zawahiri, since bin Laden's death, the head of al Qaeda."

"Go on."

"The cell leaders in each city were sent there while bin Laden was still running things, each with a lot of money, and told to do their own recruiting and training of the recruits. Al-Zawahiri has been waiting for all the cells to reach full strength and training and to select targets, then report in. Full readiness is expected sometime soon, perhaps within a month."

"Good God," Holly said.

"Quite. The head of the New York cell is also named Habib. We don't have a last name. We've no doubt that the arrival in New York of Jasmine was the catalyst that set things off there."

"Were you able to get any names of the people in the other cities?"

"We're working on that now. Something else we've learned: the setting off of the device in Los Angeles was meant to be the start of a new American and European jihad, but the failure of that effort has slowed things, and the killing of Dr. Kharl has, at least for the moment, stopped any large-scale attacks, the next of which was to be London. It is our conclusion that, without Kharl to make the devices, that effort is dead, because there is just no one else available to these people who has the requisite skills and access to materials."

"Well, that's a relief."

Kate broke in. "That's the story in a nutshell," she said. "I'm in the situation room now with the president discussing what is to be done, and Felicity is traveling to Washington almost immediately as the prime minister's representative. I am going to want your recommendations on how we should proceed."

"I can give you my recommendations now, Director," Holly said.

"I'll put you on speakerphone. Go ahead."

"After a discussion with Stone Barrington, our consultant, whose opinion I respect, I've come to the conclusion that the president should address the nation and tell them what happened in Los Angeles. If he doesn't and the story leaks, it would be much more damaging than if he tells all now. In light of what Felicity has just told us, I believe he should also reveal the existence of the al Qaeda cells in American cities and put the entire Homeland Security network on high alert. As we receive more information, the White House should release names and photographs as they come in, and we'll have the whole country looking for them. This will inevitably lead to a great many false sightings, but even that will tend to keep the country on alert."

"Thank you for that, Holly, and please thank Stone for his help. You are to transmit this information to the New York City police commissioner tomorrow morning. By that time, the FBI will have already alerted their people in New York. You have the authority to activate the situation room under the New York station for whatever use you wish. When it's up and running, you'll be able to see simultaneously whatever we're receiving in the White House situation room. We'll speak again at ten o'clock tomorrow morning. Good night."

"Good night, Director." Holly ended the connection.

"I didn't know there was a situation room under your New York building," Stone said.

"Neither did I," Holly replied. She picked up the phone. "I'm calling the commissioner."

"He'll be sound asleep."

"Not for long," she replied.

39

Holly had just reached her desk the following morning when there was a knock on her
door. She looked up to see a slim, blond
woman in her forties standing at the door.

"Good morning, Chief," the woman said.
"I'm Phyllis Schackelford. I'm section head
of Analysis, and I have an additional duty of
running our situation room downstairs.
Would you like to see it?"

"Yes, I would," Holly said.

"Please come with me." She led the way
to the elevators, and while they waited for
the car she handed Holly an odd-looking
key. "You should keep this. It will get you
all the way downstairs, and it will work in
any lock in the building."

The elevator arrived, and Phyllis indicated
four buttons, marked S1 through S4. "Sub-
basement four is the situation room," she
said. "Please insert your key in the lock next
to the button, turn it ninety degrees to the

right, then press the S4 button."

Holly turned the key, and the S4 button light came on. She pressed the button, and the elevator started down.

"We're traveling down through sixty feet of Manhattan bedrock," she said. "All the power cables and utilities are in an adjacent shaft." The elevator stopped, and the doors opened. As they did, lights came on in a vestibule. They stepped out, and the doors closed behind them.

Phyllis went to the wall to their right and opened a panel, revealing perhaps fifty switches. She inserted a key in a lock at the top and turned it to the right. All of the switches instantly repositioned themselves to the on position. Phyllis closed the panel, then walked to a pair of sliding doors and inserted her key into another lock and turned it. The doors slid open, revealing a large conference room. A wall of monitors began coming to life.

"What you're now seeing is a mirror of the displays in the White House situation room," Phyllis said.

"Can we teleconference with them from here?" Holly asked.

"Yes, from the control panel in the corner or the one at the head of the table. The two large screens at each end of the room will display the situation room. I don't want to turn them on now, because we would be simultaneously displayed on their screens."

"And you know how to operate the control panel at this end?"

"I and my assistant, Shane, are qualified. If, for any reason, we should both be unavailable, all you do is flip the master switch here" — she pointed to it — "and the operator at the White House can control this room, as well as his."

"Thank you, Phyllis." She looked at her watch. "It's seven-forty now. I'm expecting the police commissioner and the AIC of the local FBI office and some of their staffers here for a meeting at nine o'clock. Will you let garage security know that they'll be arriving, and that I've given them the code name Red Rose for admittance to the garage? We don't want a repeat of last week."

"Certainly."

"As you've no doubt heard, the president has authorized the Agency to operate domestically in terrorism cases for the remainder of his term, and he has asked Congress to make the change to our charter permanent. Who among our personnel here would be best qualified to participate in the search for the bombers?"

"I should think the three section heads in

Analysis, Operations, and Technical Services should be present at your meeting. They'll know best which of their people should be assigned to the investigation."

"Please invite them and ask them to be present at eight forty-five. I want the room to be fully staffed when the others arrive."

"Certainly. Chief. You may not be aware, but there is an office suite for the station chief on the top floor which is unoccupied, because we've never had a station chief. Since you now hold that position, you might like to move in there. May I show it to you?"

"Thank you, yes."

They rode the elevator to the top floor of the building, and Phyllis led her to the south end of the hallway and opened one of the pairs of double doors. "Your key works this lock, too," she said.

Holly walked into a large office suite that spanned the width of the building, including an office, a secretary's office, a kitchenette, and a conference room.

"The sliding doors lead to a glassed-in terrace, which is well placed to avoid surveillance or attack," Phyllis said. She opened the doors. "The glass, like all the glass in the building, is armored and triple glazed, and the outside of the windows has a coating of film which makes them mirrored, so that no one can see in. Would you like me to find you a secretary?"

Holly thought about that. "No, thank you, I have a secretary at Langley that I've hardly met. I'll have her come up here."

"We have residential quarters that can house her comfortably," Phyllis said.

"I know, I've stayed here a couple of times in the past."

"Is there anything else I can do for you before the nine o'clock meeting?"

"Yes, if you could go back to my temporary office, close my briefcase, and send someone up here with it, that would be very helpful." Phyllis left, and Holly sat down at her desk. Everything was very nice in her new office. She picked up the phone and called her secretary, Heather, known as Scotty, at Langley.

"Assistant director's office," she said.

"Scotty, it's Holly."

"Good morning, Director."

"I'm not the Director."

"It's protocol for how you are addressed, just as a lieutenant governor is addressed as 'governor.' "

"I see. I don't know what your personal situation is, but I'm about to disrupt your life."

"I'm single, and I live alone, if that's what

you mean, Director. I don't even have a cat."

"That's what I mean. I'd like you to go home, pack a couple of bags, and get yourself to the New York station by the fastest available means."

"The director is choppering up this afternoon."

"See if you can hitch a ride."

"How long will I be in New York?"

"Indefinitely. Housing will be provided."

"I'll see you this afternoon. If I have to travel commercial, I'll let you know."

"See you then, Scotty." Holly hung up. So the director was coming up, unannounced. Her phone rang. "Holly Barker."

"Holly, it's Kate. I'm coming to New York this afternoon."

"Very good, Director. May my secretary hitch a ride with you? I'm bringing her up for the duration."

"Of course. If you would have a car at the East Side Heliport for us at three, I'd appreciate it."

"Certainly, ma'am."

"And Holly, I think we know each other well enough now for us to be on a first-name basis. From now on I'm Kate, except on official occasions."

"I'm meeting with the police commissioner and the FBI's AIC and their people at nine in our situation room here. We'll be available to conference with the White House situation room, if necessary."

"Good. You may ask Stone to join you, if you wish. He's cleared for that."

"I have already done so," Holly said.

"I'm glad you're taking hold up there," Kate said.

"Thank you, Kate." They hung up, and Holly walked around her new office suite, exploring every nook and cranny.

40

At eight-thirty Holly went down to the situation room and, with the help of Phyllis Schackelford, familiarized herself with the controls on the table beside her chair. Everything was clearly labeled, but she put Phyllis at her left for the meeting, in case she needed help.

Stone arrived at eight forty-five and looked around the room. "Just like the one in the White House," he said. "Maybe a little smaller."

"Wait until you see my office," Holly whispered.

The two other section heads arrived and introduced themselves, and at the stroke of nine, the elevator doors opened, and the police commissioner and the FBI's AIC, followed by half a dozen assistants, arrived and were seated at the table.

Holly addressed them. "Good morning, ladies and gentlemen, and welcome to the first meeting of what we will call, for working purposes, the joint executive committee for New York intelligence, or EXCOM. I've asked you here to tell you what we've learned from our sources abroad and to begin to coordinate our efforts to stop these bombings and capture or kill the persons responsible for them."

She sat down. "First of all, I must tell you that a few weeks ago, at the grand opening of a hotel called The Arrington, in Los Angeles, while the presidents of the United States and Mexico were in residence, an al Qaeda group attempted to infiltrate three powerful bombs into the hotel and explode them. Through a combination of good work by the Secret Service and The Arrington's security personnel and good luck, their efforts were thwarted. Two of the team were captured, one was killed when his bomb exploded at Santa Monica Airport, and two others were killed in New York during a firefight with CIA officers. You will know about this from official reports and from the news media.

"What you don't know is that an attempt to detonate a nuclear device at the hotel was narrowly averted, again by Secret Service and private security personnel, and by Stone Barrington, who is sitting to my right." She paused to let this sink in. "The reason you have not known about this until now is that, for obvious reasons, the information was confined to only those people directly involved in the incident."

"How big a device?" the commissioner asked.

"Big enough to decimate a significant portion of Los Angeles and kill, either immediately or in the months following the blast, something like a million people."

"Jesus Christ," the commissioner said.

"Before you ask, we have good reason to believe that there is no other nuclear threat out there. There were six on the team that assembled and transported the device — three are dead, two are in custody, and a Pakistani called Dr. Kharl, who designed, obtained the materials for, and assembled the device, died in Dubai a few days later. Without him they do not have the resources to construct and deliver another such device. However, the sixth member of the team, whose name is Jasmine Shazaz, and whose brothers were the two team members who died in New York, is still active and is believed to be in the city as we speak. She is responsible for the three explosions that took place in London recently and the two explosions that have recently occurred here.

Last evening we learned from a foreign intelligence source that there are four other al Qaeda cells operating in Boston, Chicago, Los Angeles, and Atlanta, and that they are well financed and equipped.

"It is our immediate task to find and capture or kill Jasmine and her local team and to discover anything we can about the identity and location of the teams in the other cities. As you know, the president has authorized the CIA to work domestically on this and other cases of terrorism for the duration of his second term, and he has asked the Congress to change the Agency's charter to that effect."

The AIC spoke up. "I should tell you that the Bureau objects in the strongest terms to this action by the president," he said. "We believe his executive order to be unconstitutional and we will urge the Congress not to alter the Agency's charter and open up that can of worms. We have the intelligence resources and the staffing to uncover and counter any terroristic threat to this country."

"I'm sorry, Agent, but if that were true you would have known that al Qaeda teams were operating in five major American cities," Holly said.

"Exactly right," the commissioner interjected. "Why do you think we have such a large antiterrorist unit in our city?"

"Gentlemen, I don't want this to devolve into internecine warfare. What we have to do is too important to have interagency rivalries damage our efforts. I suggest that it is the obligation of all of us to follow the president's executive order until such time as the courts might overrule it."

"Are you going to be flooding this city with CIA agents on the ground?" the AIC asked.

"I expect we will have a few people brought in, but I regard our primary purpose as one of intelligence. We simply don't have the manpower to do what the commissioner can do, with his thousands of officers, and we have no wish to interfere with any investigation the FBI is currently running."

"Well," the AIC said, "I guess that's the best we can hope for."

The commissioner spoke up. "Exactly what would you like my department to do?"

"Our intelligence tells us that the New York cell is quartered in an apartment or house somewhere on the West Side of Manhattan. We would like you to act on that intelligence by putting as many people as you can into the West Side, distributing the only photograph we have of Jasmine to every shop, restaurant, and bar. This is now a manhunt, and the NYPD is the best agency to lead it."

"I can do that," the commissioner said.

"And what would you like the Bureau to do?" the AIC asked archly.

"We'd like you to contact every source of intelligence that you possess, every agent, every snitch, and enlist them in the hunt for Jasmine."

Stone spoke up. "May I make a suggestion?" he asked.

"Certainly," Holly replied.

"Since these people will know that we're looking for them, they will hole up and hunker down, and they're going to have to eat. Since they are of Middle Eastern origin, I suggest you contact every Middle Eastern or Indian restaurant on the West Side that delivers meals, and find out if any of their deliverymen has seen Jasmine."

"I'm sorry," the AIC said, "but I don't know who you are, Mr. . . . ah, Harrington?"

"Barrington."

"I believe I can answer that," the commissioner said. "Stone is a retired NYPD detective first grade who is now a prominent New York City attorney, with the firm of Woodman & Weld."

"And," Holly added, "Mr. Barrington has for some years been a consultant to the Agency, and we have found his advice to be very useful on several occasions. You should also know that, in London, a very important arrest was made a couple of days ago because a milkman recognized Jasmine from a photograph circulated to his company, so do not discount restaurant deliverymen."

"She's right," the commissioner said, "and Stone knows a lot more about this city than you do, Agent. I think his suggestion is an excellent one, exhibiting just the kind of thinking that will help us find these people."

"Let's continue," Holly said.

41

After the meeting had adjourned Holly took Stone back to her new office. "What do you think?" she asked, waving an arm.

"Beautiful," he said.

"I didn't even know it existed until this morning. Since we've never had a station chief here, nobody used it." Her phone rang. "Holly Barker."

"It's Lance," her former boss said. "Bring me up to date."

Holly told him the details of what had occurred during the past twenty-four hours.

"What can I do to help?"

"You can contact every station chief who runs informants and find out what you can about the cells in the five American cities. Have them pump the local intelligence services for information. What we know now we got from MI-6. There may be some knowledge drifting in the wind."

"I'll start on that immediately. It's the

kind of thing I'd have ordered you to do a few weeks ago."

"Isn't your new deputy working out?"

"He'll do, but he's not you."

"That's the highest praise I've ever had from you, Lance."

"And well deserved. By the way, congratulations on the station chief's job."

"Thank you."

"I'll get back to you when I have something to get back to you with."

"Bye." They both hung up.

"Your FBI guest behaved just like every other agent I've had to work with," Stone said.

"I think they have a couple of courses at Quantico on how to be a pain in the ass."

"I think you're right to involve him as little as possible, and I'll be very surprised if he comes up with any useful information. The Bureau doesn't like running snitches — they don't like to associate with the lower types."

"The commissioner doesn't like him any better than I do," Holly said. "It's the NYPD who are going to find Jasmine."

"I think you're right," Stone said.

Across town Habib let himself into the basement apartment and found Jasmine watching a soap opera. He handed her the early

268

edition of the *New York Post*. "You're all over the papers," he said.

"Do you have a reliable hairdresser on your short list of people you trust most?"

"I do," Habib replied.

"I think a late-night appointment with him or her would be of great use."

"Tonight?"

"The sooner the better. I don't want to venture out in daylight until I've made that photo in the papers useless. When I'm done, I want new passport photos taken, and the appropriate adjustments made in my travel documents."

"I'll take care of that myself," he said.

"And I'm hungry. Let's order in."

"I'll get some menus," Habib said, heading for the kitchen.

Holly and Stone were having a sandwich in her office when the commissioner called.

Holly pressed the speaker button. "Good afternoon."

"I've emptied out the police academy," he said. "I've got every cadet on the West Side now, stuffing every mailbox with the photo of Jasmine, and they're paying particular attention to Middle Eastern and Indian restaurants."

"That's great news, Commissioner, and a

good use of your available manpower."

"We're going to get her sooner rather than later."

"I hope you're right."

The commissioner hung up.

"That's a good idea," Stone said.

"Yeah, the FBI would never have thought of that." She looked at her watch. "The director should be here in an hour or so, along with my new secretary, who'll be here for the duration."

"You want me to put her up at my house? I've got guest rooms available."

"No, there are rooms here, and if she finds that depressing she can use my apartment, which is just sitting there, biodegrading."

"As you wish."

Habib paid the deliveryman, brought the two paper bags into the apartment, and unpacked the containers on the dining table.

Jasmine helped herself to the various dishes. "I feel like I'm in Damascus," she said.

"There are good restaurants in New York," Habib said.

"Remember," Jasmine said, "I'm a Londoner, I like northern Italian food."

42

Scotty handed her bags to the co-pilot, climbed into the helicopter, and buckled up. She couldn't believe it: she was in a futuristic helicopter, sitting next to the director of Central Intelligence, about to depart for New York. The machine lifted off the pad, climbed about a hundred feet, then headed northeast, gaining speed rapidly. Shortly she had a grand view of Washington, one she had never seen from an aircraft.

"Spectacular, isn't it?" the director said.

"Yes, *ma'am,*" Scotty replied.

"I know we've met, but I don't know much about you," the director said.

"I joined the Agency four and a half years ago," Scotty said. "Before that Georgetown, for a bachelor's in public policy and a master's in foreign studies, then eight years in the State Department, working for two assistant secretaries of state."

"How are you liking the Agency?"

"Very, very much," Scotty said, "and I think I have the best job in the building, except maybe Ms. Barker's and yours."

"I'm glad you feel that way," the director said. She opened a *New York Times* and read until they were over New York City. Moments later they were exiting the chopper and climbing into a black SUV.

"Have you been to the New York station before?"

"No, ma'am, I've only been to the city twice before."

Kate Lee nodded and answered her cell phone.

Holly's phone rang. "Holly Barker."

"This is security. The director and your secretary are on the way up."

"Thank you." She hung up. "They're here," she said to Stone.

A moment later the two women bustled into the office. "Hey, I like this," Kate Lee said. "Hi, Stone."

"Hello, Director."

"Did you enjoy this morning's meeting?"

"It was enlightening," Stone replied. "Are you staying overnight?"

"Maybe."

"May we take you to dinner?"

"I'd like that. Let me check in with the

White House and see what my schedule there is like."

Holly showed Scotty her office and the kitchenette.

"I'll make coffee," Scotty said.

Kate flopped down in a chair in Holly's comfortable sitting area. "I've been on the phone with the director of the FBI," she said. "They're terribly upset over there about the expansion of our charter."

"I got that impression from the AIC," Holly said.

"I know that man, and he's an ignoranus," Kate said.

"I beg your pardon?"

"He's both stupid and an asshole."

Holly and Stone erupted in laughter. "I couldn't have characterized him better," Holly said, when she had control of herself again.

"Appear to be cooperating with the Bureau," Kate said, "but don't let it get in your way. Any news?"

"Yes, the commissioner has turned out all the students at the police academy and has them papering the West Side with flyers."

"What a great idea! I like that man." Her cell phone rang, and she answered it. "Hello, darling," she said. "I mean, hello, Mr. President. Yes, good flight. I'm with Holly and Stone. They've asked me to dinner. You need me this evening? Not for that, dummy, do we have a state dinner or anything? Good, then I'll stay over. At the Carlyle. The Secret Service likes it. Okay, I'll see you tomorrow night." She hung up. "I guess we're on for dinner. I warn you, it'll be a production — the Secret Service will be all over it."

"It'll be just the three of us," Stone said, "so why don't we dine at my house? I've got a wonderful cook, and there's already Agency security on the place."

"Sounds great. Nothing fancy, I hope."

"We'll dine in the kitchen. And I'll invite Mike Freeman, if you like."

"Wonderful! Scotty, will you let my Secret Service detail know that I'm dining at Mr. Barrington's tonight?"

"Yes, ma'am," Scotty said. "I have the address." She stepped out into the hallway for a moment, then came back with an agent.

"Mr. Barrington," the man said, "may we have a look at your home this afternoon?"

"Of course. My secretary, Joan Robertson, is there, and so is the housekeeper. I'll let them know you're coming."

"I'll be staying at the Carlyle tonight," Kate said to the man. "Will you let them know?"

"You're welcome to stay at my house," Stone said.

"Thanks, but I've got clothes and stuff at the Carlyle. What time?"

"Drinks at seven?"

"Perfect."

"Is there anybody you'd like to ask?"

"No, let's keep it small, it'll be more fun."

Stone excused himself and stepped away, digging out his cell phone.

"Woodman & Weld," Joan said.

"Hi, it's me. Will you let Helene know we'll be four for dinner this evening? Oh, and invite Mike Freeman. Drinks at seven. Adjust the numbers, if he's bringing someone."

"Of course. Do you want anything special?"

"Tell her to cook Greek. It's what she loves most, and tell her our guest is the first lady."

"Omigod! Are you sure you want her to know?"

"Maybe you're right, we'll surprise her, but you can tell Mike."

"I think that's best. What time?"

"Drinks at seven, in the garden. The Secret Service will be calling on you shortly, so give them a look around. Have them look at the garden, too. We can dine out there, if they approve."

"Okay."

"Any calls?"

"Nothing you'd want to hear about."

Stone laughed. "Okay, you can deal with those." He hung up.

"We're all set," he said to Kate.

"I'm sorry about all the Secret Service stuff. I know it's a pain in the ass."

"Not in the least. I'm happy to have the extra security in these troubled times."

"Wait until you taste Helene's cooking," Holly said.

"I feel a weight gain coming on," Kate replied.

43

Stone had Helene put a couple of extra chairs at the banquette in the big kitchen, and told her to use a linen tablecloth.

"Anybody I know coming, Mr. Stone?" Helene asked.

"Oh, I don't know, maybe. Mr. Freeman will be here — he loves your cooking."

Helene blushed.

Stone went upstairs and sat in his study while Holly changed for dinner. At a quarter to seven, the front doorbell rang. He picked up the phone: "Yes?"

"Hi, Stone, it's Mike. I'm early, I know. Will you let these guys in the SUV know not to shoot me?"

"Sure, Mike, I'll buzz you in. I'm in the study." Stone called the phone in the car and eased the minds of the two Agency security men.

Mike made his way to the study, and Stone poured him a drink. "Have a seat,

Mike. What's up?"

"I wanted to talk with you about something, and this seems like a good time."

"Sure."

"It occurs to me that, since Kate Lee has only a few months left in office, it might be good if we asked her to join the Strategic Services board."

"What a good idea!"

"Do you think she'd consider it?"

Holly spoke up from the doorway. "I think she'd jump at it." She poured herself a drink, allowed Mike to peck her on the cheek, and sat down.

"Why jump?" Mike asked.

"I think she's nervous about having enough to do when the president has left office. I know for a fact that she doesn't want to spend a lot of time on his family cattle farm. She has a horror of anything agricultural."

"I hope you're right," Mike said.

"And," Holly continued, "it would give her an excuse to spend some time in New York. She likes it here, and so does her husband."

"Then I'll broach the subject," Mike said. "There's something else: I had lunch with the AIC of the New York FBI office today, and we tiptoed around the subject of Jasmine Shazaz and her friends."

"Oh?" Holly asked. "Anything I should know about?"

"Nothing specific, but he gave me the impression that he wasn't much interested in cooperating with your people and the NYPD in the hunt. The Bureau has always been a credit hog, and I think they would prefer not to share it with anybody in this instance."

"Did he give you any indication of what his plan is?"

"Only that they're bringing in something like fifty more agents to work on it."

Stone spoke up. "I'll bet they won't be distributing flyers on the West Side."

"Anything else?" Holly asked.

"Only that, in my opinion, the AIC would do anything he could think of to derail your efforts in his favor. Did you see the piece in *The New York Times Magazine* about the Bureau's bumbling in intelligence matters over the years?"

"I did. Bumbling seems to be a tradition at the Bureau."

The doorbell rang, and Stone picked up the phone. "Yes?"

"This is Special Agent Carmichael with the Secret Service," a male voice said. "The director will arrive in two minutes."

"Thank you," Stone said. "I'll be right down to meet her. Did you identify yourself to the two men in the black SUV?"

"They insisted," the man replied.

Stone laughed and hung up. "She's on her way. I'll bring her here," he said. "Sit tight." He walked to the front door and arrived in time to see the car pull up outside. It had begun to drizzle, and the agent held an umbrella for her as she exited the car.

She ran up the steps, came inside, and gave Stone a kiss on the cheek. "What a handsome house," she said, looking around the living room.

Stone hung up her raincoat. "Thank you. It was built by my great-aunt, my grandmother's sister, and my father did all the woodwork and much of the furniture."

"He was very, very good," she said.

"Holly and Mike are in my study. Come this way." He led her into the smaller room and, while she greeted Mike and Holly, poured her a bourbon.

She flopped down on the sofa and took a sip of her drink. "This is fun already," she said. "Will and I don't get that many opportunities to dine in someone else's home, unless it's a grand occasion."

"You're very welcome here," Stone said. "I'm sorry the president couldn't join us."

"He's speaking to the Security Council at the U.N. tomorrow morning, so he's on the way up from Washington now," Kate replied. "He won't be able to make dinner, but he said he might stop in for a drink later."

"That would be wonderful. Kate, before we go down for dinner, Mike would like to speak with you about something."

"Of course," she said, taking another sip of her bourbon.

"Mrs. Lee . . ."

"Kate, please, Mike."

"Kate. It has occurred to me that you're going to be retiring from government service in the not-too-distant future."

"The Constitution insists that Will retire, and I pretty much have to go with him."

"Well, perhaps we can find a way to keep you from being bored after you are a private citizen again."

"Oh, good! I've been worried about that."

"Stone and I would like it very much if you would consider joining the board of Strategic Services."

"What an interesting idea," she replied. "What would that entail?"

"We meet more often than some boards, on the first Monday of each month, except August, when everybody seems to be out of town. Since we work our board pretty hard, the pay is twenty-five thousand per meeting, but you're certainly not required to make every one."

"Just when I need the money?"

Mike laughed. "If you're feeling flush, you can miss some meetings, but we'd like to see you there as often as possible."

"Mike, you understand that, even after I leave the Agency, I'll be under very tight strictures about what I can discuss."

"We're more interested in the experience you've acquired and in your judgment," Mike said. "And, though we like gossip as much as anyone, we're not interested in official secrets."

"That makes your offer very attractive indeed," Kate said. "I'll have to discuss it with Will, of course, but he likes New York as much as I do."

"I know you have a great deal on your plate between now and retirement, so I don't expect an immediate answer."

"Thank you. I'll think about it when I can."

The phone buzzed. "That's Helene," Stone said, "telling us to come to dinner."

44

They dined and drank wine and talked and laughed, and not once did anyone bring up the Agency, the White House, or Jasmine Shazaz.

"I don't know when I've had so much fun," Kate said, as Stone poured her more wine. "It's such a relief not to have to keep up appearances, for fear of what will be in the columns the next morning."

"This is a leakproof environment," Stone said, "and you're welcome anytime."

"It looks like you folks are having way too much fun," said a voice from the door to the kitchen. Will Lee came in and pulled up an extra chair.

"Good evening, Mr. President," Stone said.

"It's just Will in this company," he replied, accepting a glass of wine.

"Will," Kate said, "I've had a job offer."

"You already have a job," he said. "Doesn't

it keep you busy enough?"

"It will until next January," she said. "Then I'll be at loose ends."

"What's the job?"

"Mike and Stone have asked me to join the board of Strategic Services."

"Have they, now?" Will said, frowning a little.

"They have, and unless you can cough up some substantive reason why I shouldn't, I'm going to accept."

"Well, it's usually presidents who join boards in the afterlife, but I don't think there's any law against a first lady doing the same."

"Any personal objections?"

"If there were, I wouldn't air them here."

"I'm sorry," she giggled. "I have wine taken, and I'm a little giddy."

"You need to be giddy more often," Will said.

"In time."

"Take the offer," he said, "but all of you, not a word to anyone until we're well out of office. I think next spring might be a good time for an announcement."

"May I tell the other members of the board?" Mike asked.

"You may not. It will be a nice surprise for them." Will turned to his wife. "Well, we

284

have an excuse to keep the apartment at the Carlyle instead of looking for something cheaper."

"I'll pick up the maintenance on the place," Kate said.

"I may take you up on that," Will said. He raised his glass. "Congratulations to all of you."

A car pulled up in front of a shop in Soho, and Habib got out and rapped on the glass door. It was unlocked by a woman, and Habib went back to the car and opened the door for Jasmine, who ran inside.

"I'll park the car," Habib said, then left. "I'll be back in . . . how long?"

"That depends on what you wish done," the woman said. She was of Middle Eastern extraction, tall, with long black hair pulled up in a bun.

"Shampoo, cut, coloring," Jasmine said.

"Two hours," the woman said to Habib, who left, closing the door behind him.

"My name is Sheba," the woman said, locking the door. "Please come through."

They left the handsome reception room and went into the rear of the building, where hairdressers' booths were set up, then through a door off the larger room. "This is my private room," Sheba said, waving her to the chair. "Let's talk about what you need." She stood behind Jasmine and looked at her in the mirror while she talked.

"I want it shorter, but not too short," Jasmine said. "Do you think I have the skin for blond hair?"

"I have the perfect blond shade for your skin," Sheba replied. "With blonder highlights. You'll love it."

"I'm in your hands, then," Jasmine said.

"Come, let me wash your hair."

Jasmine moved to the other chair and lay back, resting her neck on the shaped edge of the sink while Sheba gently shampooed and rinsed her hair.

Sheba dried it with a towel, then moved her client back to the other chair and began to cut it quickly, shaping as she went. Finally, she stopped. "How's that for length?" she asked.

"Excellent," Jasmine replied.

"Now let's begin on the color."

The president looked at his watch. "Good God!"

"Time flies when you're having fun," Kate said.

"I was going to read through my speech again before bedtime," Will said, "but the hell with it. It can wait until breakfast." He got to his feet.

"Thanks so much for keeping my wife off the streets," he said, "and for the promise of work for her later. I've always told her she'd have to support me in my old age."

"We're looking forward to having her aboard," Mike said.

"And I was looking forward to having her to myself," Will said. "So much for that."

"Oh, I think I can work you into my schedule," Kate said. They walked up the stairs, and Will produced a cell phone and pressed a button. "Now," he said.

Stone opened the front door and looked up and down the block. All was quiet, only a couple of Secret Service men standing by. Then, from around a corner, a procession of four black SUVs drove slowly into the block and stopped.

Everybody shook hands with Will and kissed Kate, and they were gone.

"Come on back to the study for a brandy," Stone said.

"You two boys besot yourselves," Holly said. "I'm hitting the sack — nothing but big days ahead." She disappeared into the elevator.

Stone and Mike went back to the study and found cognac.

"Well, that was a surprise," Mike said,

"Kate's blurting it out like that. I thought she'd take weeks to think it over."

"She knows her husband very well," Stone said. "She took the moment."

"I'm delighted she did."

"So am I. She's a remarkable person, and she'll fit right into the board."

"I'm going to go after Holly, too," Mike said. "But for an executive position, not the board, and not just yet."

"You won't get an argument from me," Stone said, "and I think she'll want it. When Kate goes, she'll be adrift in the Agency. She doesn't have the stature yet to be director, and the alternative is to go back to work for Lance Cabot again, and she's been there, done that."

"Pretty much what I figured," Mike said, raising his glass.

Jasmine sat in the chair and looked at her new hairstyle and color. "It's perfect," she said.

"Perfection is what we deal in," Sheba replied. "The change in the eyebrows will help give you a new appearance, too. As it is, you look nothing like the person in the flyers that are all over town."

So she knew whom she was dealing with, Jasmine thought. She stood up. "How much do I owe you?" she asked, reaching for her purse.

"One hundred thousand dollars," Sheba replied calmly. "Our special price for fugitives."

Jasmine laughed. "And worth every penny," she said. If she wanted that much now, what would she demand when the reward was offered? She reached into her purse, and her hand closed on the butt of the Walther PPK, silencer fitted. In one easy motion, she turned, raised the little pistol, and fired into Sheba's face. A small hole appeared on one side of her forehead, and blood trickled down her face.

Sheba looked astonished, and seemed to be trying to speak, but she didn't fall; she clutched at a countertop to steady herself.

Jasmine shot her in the head again, and Sheba collapsed in a heap at her feet.

Back in the car, Habib spoke. "You look wonderful," he said. "Did you kill her?"

"She wanted a hundred thousand dollars," Jasmine replied. "Can you believe it? We would never have been able to trust her."

"Quite right," Habib said, and drove away.

45

The New York City police commissioner was having a sandwich at his desk and enjoying some unaccustomed solitude when his secretary buzzed. He picked up the phone. "I'm deep into corned beef and chicken liver at the moment," he said. "Do you have something more important than that for me?"

"I have the chief of detectives for you, Commissioner — in the flesh."

"Oh, shit, send him in, then."

The man ambled into the commissioner's office. "I've got an interesting homicide," he said.

"As I recall, you get something like two-point-seven homicides a week, Dan."

"Not many of them are as interesting as this one," the chief replied.

The commissioner took a huge bite of his sandwich, put it down, and beckoned for the file as he chewed. He opened it and read the first page, then grabbed the diet soda and washed things down. "A hairdresser, shot twice in the head? What is it, some sort of high-fashion mob hit?"

"The hairdresser was known as Sheba, and she had a very fat client list of women of Middle Eastern background." The chief paused, but the commissioner still didn't seem to get it. "She is also renowned for turning her clients into blondes."

The commissioner took another swig of his diet soda and pondered this, then his bushy eyebrows shot up. "Holy shit!"

"I thought you would say something like that. One of her employees told our detective that she was the last one out of the shop, at around nine last evening, and that Sheba — that is apparently her only name — locked the door behind her. This morning at seven forty-five, when she showed up for work, the door was unlocked. She had a look around and found nothing amiss, then she thought to look in the private room where Sheba took her personal customers and found her on the floor, with two bullet wounds to the head. Coroner reckons she died between ten and twelve last night. Sheba was not known for having customers after closing time — she was always out by eight or nine."

"Anything interesting in the way of prints?"

"I thought you'd ask. Normally, everything would be wiped down by the cleaning lady, but Sheba called her yesterday and gave her the night off. The place is a swamp of prints, and we're running them as we lift them, directly from the scene."

"Ah, electronics!" said the commissioner, who had spent one hell of a lot of the city's money on such gadgetry.

"Ah, indeed. So far we've identified a woman with a record of shoplifting and matched another set to those found at a burglary in the neighborhood two weeks ago. No name, so the burglar doesn't have an arrest record anywhere." The chief cleared his throat. "And the prints of one man."

"Come on, tell me."

"His name is Habib Johnson."

"What, an Arab Swede?"

"Exactly. Arab mother, Swedish father, born in Brooklyn thirty-three years ago, earns his living from a small-time bookkeeping business, with a list of Arab and Arab-American clients."

"Can we connect him to anything?"

"He was questioned late last year in an investigation of a gun-running ring operating between Virginia and here, but he was released without charges. He knew some of those involved, but we didn't have enough evidence to connect him to the gun sales."

"Have you picked him up yet?"

"He wasn't at his office or his home, but his secretary said that wasn't unusual. He's apparently out and about most days."

"Track his cell phone."

"We tried — no dice."

"I haven't said this in years," the commissioner said, "but put out an APB on the son of a bitch, and I want to watch the interrogation."

"Yes, sir."

"And, Dan, circulate to all officers that Jasmine may be a blonde now, but don't release that to the public. I don't want her to know we know."

"Yes, sir."

The commissioner's phone buzzed again. "What?" He listened for a moment. "Thank you." He hung up again. "The FBI has finally done something right," he said.

"You're kidding me."

"Nope. They've offered a five-million-dollar reward for information leading to the capture — with no mention of conviction — of Jasmine Shazaz."

"That's unusual," the chief said.

"It certainly is," the commissioner replied. "They might as well have said 'Dead or alive.' "

46

Holly was meeting with a restaurant designer, who was showing her drawings of the way the new station dining room would look, when Scotty buzzed her. "The police commissioner for you."

Holly handed the drawings back to the designer. "It looks great. How soon?"

"All the fixtures are available ready-made. Three days?"

"Go. Now I have to take a call." The man left, and Holly pressed the button. "Commissioner?"

"Holly, I have interesting news."

Holly listened with growing excitement to the story of the dead hairdresser. "Any luck finding Habib?"

"Not yet," the commissioner said.

"Will you keep me posted?"

"Certainly."

"Oh, and, Commissioner, please remember that this woman has a history of booby-trapping a premises when abandoning it."

"I remember the report from London."

"And MI-6 tells us that she probably detonated the bomb from within sight of the house."

"That's scary — makes it more difficult for us to get inside. A booby trap would be easier."

"When you find her hiding place, you have to pour officers into the block and check every single person before sending men in."

"I'll do that." The commissioner said good-bye and hung up.

Scotty appeared before her. "The chef that was recommended is here for his interview."

"Scotty, will you interview him? I'm in over my head here. Take him downstairs and show him the dining room and the kitchen. Show him the drawings the designer brought, too. Tell him we want high-end comfort food on the menu and small portions. I don't want everybody to start gaining weight, especially me."

"Yes, ma'am," Scotty said, and left the room.

Habib let himself into the apartment and found Jasmine in the living room, pointing a gun at him.

"You should call first," she said.

"I'm afraid to use my cell phone," he replied. "The police have been to my office and interrogated my employees. They will certainly try to track my cell phone."

"How did they get on to you?"

"I've no idea. I've been racking my brain about that."

Jasmine dug into her bag and produced a throwaway phone. "This is good for a hundred hours," she said. "When it runs low, buy a couple more."

"Right. And now I have to move in here."

"That seems sensible," Jasmine said. "After all, there are three bedrooms. Take the one farthest from mine."

"Thank you. I will."

"What are you driving?"

"A rental car."

"In your own name?"

"Yes."

"Take it to a neighborhood you don't frequent, wipe it down, and abandon it."

"But the rental car company will —"

"You don't get it, do you, Habib? You're a fugitive — you don't deal with rental car companies unless you're using false ID."

"I'm sorry, what I meant by my own name was the ID I'm using."

"Shred it and manufacture a new one, and make it good."

"Right."

"Habib, I think we're both going to have to leave New York soon. We're getting too hot."

"I can do that."

"You have cash?"

"Yes."

"Buy a good used car and register it in the name of your new ID. I think we're going to have to travel by car."

"Travel where?"

"I haven't decided yet, but we need to hook up with one of the other teams around the country."

"Can we go to Los Angeles?"

"Why?"

Habib looked sheepish. "I've always wanted to see Hollywood."

Jasmine laughed. "Sure, why not L.A.? It's far enough away. We'll drive a few hundred miles, then take a plane."

"I'll get rid of the car," he said.

"Don't go back to where you live. Consider that place abandoned. Buy some new clothes and a suitcase."

"Right. Can I get you anything while I'm out?"

"Yes. Get me a couple of bottles of Chivas Regal scotch and some soda water."

"All right."

"I think you'd better shave your beard, too."

"Can I keep the mustache?"

"No. You have a New York driver's license, don't you?"

"Yes."

"And your picture is with the beard?"

"Yes."

"They'll be using that photo," Jasmine said. "You don't want to look anything like it. Get a short haircut, too."

"All right."

"Get going, then."

Habib got going.

Jasmine read the paper for a while, then suddenly she saw herself staring at her own face on the TV, at New York 1, the local news service. The volume was turned down, and she turned it up.

". . . woman is being sought all over the city by the police and the FBI. The FBI has announced a reward of five million dollars for information leading to her capture."

Jasmine turned off the set. She had been expecting this, but not such a high number. Now she could only leave the house for missions — no strolling around the city, even with blond hair.

47

Holly got out of the SUV in front of James Rutledge's building, rang the bell, and was buzzed up.

Kelli Keane answered the door. "Hi, Holly, come on in," she said.

Holly surrendered her coat but kept her briefcase. "What a beautiful place," she said as they walked through the kitchen to the living room.

"It's what Jim does," Kelli said. "He uses the apartment as a showcase for prospective clients. They're always impressed. I was surprised to get your call."

"Isn't Jim here?"

"Any minute," Kelli replied. "He's on the way home from a job."

"May I see the bedroom?"

"Of course. Right this way."

Holly walked into the big room and checked the corners for her cameras; no sign of them. She smiled inside. "Beautiful."

"Thank you. I helped with this room."

They went back into the living room in time to greet Jim, who was tossing his coat onto a bar stool in the kitchen. He greeted Holly. "What can I get you to drink?"

"Nothing, thanks, I'm here on business." She looked at Kelli and saw the change in her face.

"Business?" Jim asked. "Are you thinking of buying a place in New York, Holly?"

"I already have a place in New York," Holly said. "No, this is CIA business. Sit down, please."

Jim was looking at Kelli, worried now.

"Kelli, you will recall our previous conversation about events when you were in L.A." It wasn't a question.

Kelli nodded, but seemed unable to speak.

"Apparently, you did not keep your word to me — you were unable to contain yourself."

"Now, wait a minute —" Jim said.

"Shut up and listen," Holly said to both of them. She removed a file folder from her briefcase and extracted three official-looking documents from it, handing each of them a copy. "This is a federal court order," Holly said. "Read it."

Kelli didn't even glance at it. "Just tell me what it says."

"It says that the two of you are permanently enjoined from ever speaking to anyone, even each other, about the events in L.A. If you do so, you will be arrested and charged with criminal contempt of court, which will allow a judge to detain you in jail for as long as he deems necessary, and without a trial. Do you understand that?"

Both Jim and Kelli were staring at her, speechless.

"How did you know?" Jim asked. "Kelli, did you tell anyone but me about this?"

Kelli shook her head. "No, I didn't, and I'd like to know how you knew about our conversation, Holly."

"You aren't entitled to know that," Holly said. "Now I want you both to read the court order — all of it — right now."

The two of them read through the two-page document.

"All right," Jim said, "we've read it."

"Good. Do you now understand your position with regard to this information and the court?"

"I suppose so," Jim said.

Kelli nodded again. "Yes, I understand."

"Good." Holly opened the third document

and placed it on the coffee table, along with her pen. "Now read this document, which says that you have read and understand the court order and that you will obey it. You also agree not to consult counsel either now or if you are arrested. Do you understand?"

They both nodded.

"Now, sign the document."

Both did so.

Holly sat up, returned the documents to her briefcase, and snapped it shut. "It's time you understood who and what you're dealing with. It's possible that information about the events in L.A. may soon be made public, but the injunction permanently enjoins you from discussing or writing about them, even if they are made public. That is your punishment, Kelli, for breaking your word. You have the most important news story since nine-eleven, and you cannot write it, ever."

Holly got up, walked back to the front door, retrieved her coat, and left them standing in their living room, closing the door sharply behind her.

When they were alone, Jim wheeled on Kelli. "What the hell —"

Kelli held up a hand. "Be quiet," she said. "We're being listened to, and this time it's not that tabloid rag."

"You mean the CIA has wired our apartment?"

Kelli nodded. "It just hit me, when I was showing her the bedroom. She was looking up at the corners of the room. That guy who came and took out the old bugs? He wasn't sent by Herb Fisher's girlfriend — he was sent by Holly Barker."

"How do you know that?"

"I just do. I figured it out. I'm not stupid, although it was stupid of me to tell you anything."

"I haven't mentioned it to anybody," he protested.

"No, and that's how I know we're wired, because neither of us has ever discussed it with anybody but each other, and in our bedroom. And yet Holly knows we did that."

Jim went and poured two stiff drinks, then returned and gave Kelli one. "Then let's stop talking about it right now and never bring it up again, just like the court order says." He took a swig of his whiskey. "This never happened, any of it, do you understand? Not L.A., not our conversation, not Holly's visit. None of it. Agreed?"

Kelli took a gulp of her own drink. "Agreed. It never happened."

■ ■ ■ ■

Holly got home and found Stone in his study. He poured them a drink. "How was your day?"

"Satisfying," Holly replied.

"How so?"

"I took care of the Kelli Keane problem."

"Did you get the court order?"

"No, that turned out to be too complicated, before Congress changes our charter."

"Then how did you handle it?"

"It probably won't surprise you to learn that the Agency has people at work who can create all sorts of documents."

"Wait a minute: Are you telling me that you produced a fake court order?"

"All I'm telling you is that the Agency is capable of doing so, and we may have an acquaintance with a friendly judge who will give the correct answers if he receives an inquiry about such a thing."

"God, I wish I had a judge like that — and a forger, too. It would be so much easier to get court orders!"

48

They were on their second drink when
Holly said, "Turn on the TV."

Stone reached for the remote. "What
channel?"

"Any channel with an evening news."

Stone picked CBS. As the set came to
light, the anchorman gazed into the camera.
"In just about a minute, the president of
the United States will address the nation.
We don't know the subject of the address,
but we have assembled a panel that includes
our White House correspondent, our military adviser, and a former member of the
administration to discuss what he has to
say." He pressed a finger to his earpiece.
"Are we ready? Ladies and gentlemen, the
president of the United States."

Will Lee appeared on-screen from the
Oval Office, not sitting behind his desk as
in the usual presidential address, but standing and leaning on it, facing the camera.

"Good evening," he said. "I want to take a brief moment to pass along some information to the nation. What I'm about to tell you will be all I will have to say on the subject. I ask for your understanding on that, because we must preserve our posture on national security without telling our enemies too much.

"Recently, an attempt was made by al Qaeda to place and detonate a nuclear device in our country. The location will remain classified, but I'm glad to tell you that, because of cooperation among our intelligence services, agents of the Secret Service and others were able to learn of the plot, find the device, and disable it. The plot was attempted by a small cell of al Qaeda operatives, which included a foreign expert in the design of bombs. You should know that al Qaeda no longer has the capability of carrying out such an attack, because all the people who were a part of the plot, including the designer and builder of the device, were killed while resisting arrest — all but one."

A passport photo appeared on-screen. "This woman is Jasmine Shazaz. She is of Middle Eastern origin and was educated in Britain, and she is the chief suspect in a series of recent bombing attacks in London and New York. She has no capability of building a nuclear device, but she does have access to powerful explosives, and she is being sought by the CIA, the FBI, and the New York City Police Department as we speak. A five-million-dollar reward has been offered for information leading to her capture, and anyone with information concerning her whereabouts may telephone the toll-free number displayed on the screen and offer that information with the assurance of anonymity.

"Besides New York, she may have contacts in the following cities: Boston, Chicago, Los Angeles, and Atlanta, so citizens in those cities should be watchful. She is certain to be carrying false identification papers, and it is possible that she has taken steps to change her appearance.

"I wanted you all to know that your security forces are working hard and effectively to protect the nation from such plots, and that, once again, we have foiled and weakened al Qaeda. Thank you for your attention and good night."

The anchorman came back to the screen. "Well, that was a breathtaking announcement," he said. "Anybody have any thoughts about why the president went public with this?"

"Scott," the White House correspondent said, "I'm inclined to think that he made the announcement because he thought the story might break anyway, and he wanted to get out in front of it. And that's just what he has done. I think it's reassuring that the president seemed so relaxed in saying what he did — not even sitting behind the Oval Office desk. He seemed perfectly comfortable and confident. And I have to say that I can't remember any time, ever, that a president has promoted a manhunt — or, in this case, a womanhunt — for a fugitive terrorist. I expect they must want her very badly."

The anchorman nodded. "And I expect that the president's participation will make it much harder for this terrorist to elude the authorities. Her photograph has already been widely circulated in New York, and the president has just made it impossible for her to feel safe anywhere in the United States. Every law enforcement officer, airline ticket agent, and gas station attendant in the country is going to be checking every face that appears before him, not to mention ordinary citizens who are interested in collecting a five-million-dollar reward."

Stone switched off the TV. "Well, he was

right, it was a breathtaking announcement. I expect Kelli Keane is already on the phone to her editor, dictating her story."

"No, she isn't," Holly said. "The court order permanently enjoined her from ever speaking or writing about the events in L.A., and right this minute, I can assure you, she is wringing her hands and bemoaning her fate."

"How about Jim Rutledge?"

"He was enjoined as well, and they both took it seriously. I have it on good authority that, after I left their apartment, they swore never to discuss the events with anybody, even with each other."

"And how could you know that?"

"Let's just say that there was a witness to their conversation." She set down her glass. "I'm hungry," she said. "Let's go out for some dinner."

"We'll celebrate," Stone said, joining her.

49

Habib watched from across the street as a man and a woman left the Turtle Bay house and hailed a cab. He sat in a parked black Lincoln Town Car, hundreds of which infested the streets of Manhattan and the suburbs, and many of which could be hailed and taken anywhere. The owner of this particular car rested uneasily in the trunk, bound and gagged, as Habib started the car and fell in behind the taxicab.

The journey led past the black SUV, with government plates, parked in front of the house, around the block to Third Avenue, then uptown, past Bloomingdale's a block or two, where it stopped and disgorged its passengers into an Italian restaurant called Isle of Capri.

Holly looked around as they were seated. "Somehow it feels like an earlier decade," she said. "Late twentieth century."

"It's one of the last family-owned Italian restaurants alive in this city. There are two, maybe three generations at work here."

The owner came and greeted them and, with their drinks, a waiter brought chunks of Parmigiano-Reggiano, olives, and a jug of extra virgin olive oil and balsamic vinegar.

"There's enough here for dinner," Holly said.

"Think of it as your first course."

"Is the veal good?" she asked.

"*Everything* is good," Stone replied. "Order whatever you feel like."

"I feel like veal, maybe the piccata."

"Good choice. I'm having the osso buco, in memory of Elaine."

"That's where we would be now, isn't it? If she were still alive?"

"Certainly. It used to be that we didn't have to think of a place to dine, we just went to Elaine's. I went to her memorial service at a concert hall on the West Side last November, and Bill Bratton told a wonderful story about her."

"Bratton, the former police commissioner under Giuliani?"

"Right — the one Giuliani forced out because he was getting the credit for his own work, which was making New York the safest big city in the world. Giuliani hated

312

that he went to Elaine's, because Bill's picture would turn up on Page Six along with a description of what a great job he was doing, and that drove Giuliani crazy.

"Anyway, on Bill's last day at work, Giuliani stopped by his office and gave him the key to the city. Bill and his wife, Rikki, were headed to Elaine's for dinner with friends, and Elaine sat down with them and asked what was in the box on the table.

"Bill told her that Giuliani had given him the key to the city. She opened the box, looked at the key, and said, 'I'll bet the son of a bitch has already changed the locks!' "

"Oh, that sounds just like her!" Holly said, laughing.

Habib, looking through the restaurant window, saw the couple perusing the menu, and he got back into the Lincoln and drove back to Turtle Bay. The black SUV was still parked in front of the house, and its two occupants were reading newspapers.

He double-parked the Lincoln two blocks away and got a cab back to the West Side. Not wanting to get shot, he phoned Jasmine as he got out of the cab. "I'm home, honey," he said. "Don't blow my head off." He inserted his key and let himself into the apartment.

Jasmine looked up from her *Wall Street Journal.* "Hey, you look great without the beard. How'd it go this evening?"

"Problematical," Habib replied. "Do you know this Turtle Bay?"

"No."

"I Googled it. It's a neighborhood on the East Side that includes the United Nations, which is built on land created when the old Turtle Bay was filled in. Turtle Bay Gardens, which is where this Barrington lives, is a fashionable enclave of town houses built around a common garden. The actress Katharine Hepburn used to live in one of them. And this CIA woman, Holly Barker, is living there. We can't get at her in the CIA building, but we can get at her at this house."

"So, what kind of target is it?"

"The security on the place is holding. There are two men in a black SUV apparently permanently stationed out front, and our one successful foray into the garden turned up a man stationed at the rear door."

"What are its vulnerabilities?" Jasmine asked.

"There is an office on the ground floor. If we could get past the security and the house's security system and pack it with explosives, it would bring the house down, along with the one next door, as well, but we can't breach the outside door while those two agents are guarding the front of the house."

"I have an idea," Jasmine said, and she told him what it was.

"That could work," Habib said. "But it would have to be in the middle of the night, and we'd have to block traffic at the corner for a short time, in order to accomplish what you want."

"Where would the Barker woman and Barrington be in the middle of the night?"

"In bed at the upper rear of the house, I reckon. But if we brought down the building, they'd come down with it."

"That's the idea," Jasmine said.

50

Jasmine woke up having discovered and, perhaps, solved a problem while she slept. She showered and dressed and walked into the living room, where Habib was having breakfast.

"I like the short haircut," she said, joining him at the table and helping herself to the food.

"So do I," Habib replied, running his fingers over his smooth face. "I don't know why I didn't do this sooner."

"It's a good thing you waited," she said. "Made it easier to make a big change in your appearance."

"I expect you're right."

"I thought about the Turtle Bay house last night," she said.

"And?"

"We have to rethink it."

"Why?"

"The way it's set up now, we have to kill

the two guards in the SUV out front, which may not be as easy as we think." She held up a hand to stop him before she was interrupted. "And then we have to get the downstairs office door open quickly, which also may not be as easy as we think, and then we need to set up the device inside, run, then detonate it."

"So?"

"Houses like that come with security systems, perhaps even very elaborate security systems. What does this guy Barrington do?"

"He has a cover as a lawyer, but he's CIA."

"How do you know that?"

"Because the assistant director of the CIA is living there with him."

"Habib, did it ever occur to you that they may just be fucking?"

Habib stopped eating. "No," he said. "A prominent woman like that?"

"Your thinking is very old-fashioned," Jasmine said. "Prominent women need sex just as much as everyone else."

"Well, we have a photograph of him entering the CIA office building with her. That says to me that he's CIA."

"Okay, so he's CIA, but that helps make my point. If he is with the Agency, that house is going to be a fortress. Look at what happened when we tried to blow up the CIA building — almost nothing."

"Do you have a solution to this problem?"

"How much of the plastique do we have left after the other two explosives?"

"A little over a hundred kilos."

"That's about two hundred and fifty pounds."

"Yes, enough for many more jobs. We used only a kilo on the restaurant explosion."

"Then we'll use all of it for the Turtle Bay job."

Habib's jaw dropped. "Are you serious?"

"Entirely. How do we move it?"

"In a van. It's in one-kilo blocks. We'd pack them into boxes holding about ten kilos and stack them together."

"How do we detonate them all at once?"

"The detonators we have will set off a kilo block, then the resulting shock and heat from that explosion would be more than sufficient to set off the whole lot. It would happen so fast as to seem like one huge explosion."

"And we can set off the one-kilo explosion with a cell phone?"

"Correct. The small electrical charge is enough to set off the blasting cap or detonator, which sets off the plastique."

"I see."

"Do you? I mean, do you have any idea what a hundred kilos of that stuff will do?"

"A very great deal, I should think."

"It will take out not only Barrington's house but at least half the houses in the block. Maybe *all* the houses in the block. The fireball created would set anything standing on fire."

"How do we get it in place?"

"We drive a van into the block, already loaded and prepared, then we retreat several blocks away and call the number of the cell phone connected to the detonator."

"Or we have a suicide bomber do it."

"I'm not sure that the people available to us can be trusted to go through with it."

"The others did it."

"We used the best candidates first."

"All right, we don't need them, we'll do it ourselves."

"It's entirely possible," Habib said.

"We set it off from our escape car, then we head west."

"All right," Habib said.

"You still sound doubtful."

"It's just that I've never made and detonated a bomb this big before."

"The bigger the bomb, the bigger the effect," she said.

"If you like."

Jasmine smiled. "I like."

51

Lance Cabot stood on the far side of the Oval Office from the president's desk and listened as he made his address to the nation. Once again, he was impressed at how Will Lee could project informality and sincerity in a talk on television. The president always spoke perfect standard English but still managed to engender an intimacy with his audience. Lance noted that there was no teleprompter present. Finally, he said good night, and a moment later the lights were turned off and the crew began removing equipment from the large room.

Kate Lee, who had been standing closer to her husband, in the doorway to his secretary's office, walked over, kissed him on the lips, and whispered a few words in his ear, then the two of them, holding hands, walked across the room to where Lance stood.

"That was a remarkable job, Mr. President," Lance said, offering his hand.

"Thank you, Lance. Hungry?"

"Yes, sir."

"Then let's head up to the quarters."

"After you, sir." Lance followed them out of the Oval Office and to the elevator. Once in the living room of the quarters, the president shucked off his jacket, and Lance was surprised to see that his shirt was soaked through with sweat.

"Let me slip into something more comfortable, and I'll be right back," the president said, then left the room.

"Let me get you a drink, Lance," Kate said. "We'll be having one."

"A scotch on the rocks would be welcome, ma'am."

"A blend or a single malt? We have, let's see, Laphroaig and Glenfiddich."

"The Laphroaig would be just fine."

Kate poured the drink, then poured two bourbons and handed Lance his drink. "You're not married, are you, Lance? How come?"

"Oh, I've had a couple of close brushes, but I've managed to stay out of serious trouble."

Kate laughed. "That's what Will used to say before I got him into serious trouble. Got a girl? Or a boyfriend?"

"A girlfriend. She lives with me most of the time."

"Good for you. By the way, I was kidding about the boyfriend."

"I know, ma'am." She liked to needle him once in a while.

The president returned to the living room wearing khakis, a sport shirt, and loafers, then accepted the drink from his wife. "That's better," he said, sipping the bourbon. "I allow myself one before dinner. You never know when I might have to make a complicated decision." He waved Lance to a chair. "Make yourself comfortable, Lance. Dinner will be another half an hour."

Lance slipped into a soft armchair, and the first couple sat on the sofa facing him. He noticed that they sat close together rather than at opposite ends. It was the first time he had dined in the family quarters, and he was surprised how at ease they were with each other.

Kate poked Will in the ribs. "Speak," she said.

"Oh, yes, I almost forgot — must be the bourbon. Lance, I've decided to appoint you director of Central Intelligence."

Lance nearly dropped his drink. He had thought this might be an interview, but he hadn't expected an outright offer. This

323

meant that Kate must be stepping down. "I accept, Mr. President, with gratitude."

"Good. Got that out of the way. Your turn, sweetheart."

"Here's how it's going to go," Kate said. "First, we have to get this Jasmine thing out of the way. When that's done, I'll resign, and Will will appoint you. He'll announce the two things simultaneously in a small ceremony in the White House briefing room, on live TV."

Lance nodded. "Yes, I should think you'd want Jasmine behind you before you step down." He wanted it that way, too; he definitely did not wish to inherit that problem.

The president spoke up again. "I've spoken with Senator Jeff Barnes, whom you know from your occasional testimony before the Senate Select Committee on Intelligence, and he sees no obstacle to a smooth confirmation process. By appointing a career professional we take politics out of the equation, so there should be little if any opposition from across the aisle. And, of course, we need only Senate confirmation."

"I understand, sir."

"Both Kate and I admire the way you've conducted yourself since becoming deputy director for operations," the president said, "and I mean that as much for how you've dealt with Senator Barnes and his committee as for the operations you've conducted. The committee is well versed in how you've handled that part of your job, and because virtually everything you've done is classified, there won't be any public testimony. I expect questioning will be mostly on what sort of future you see for the Agency, especially the new domestic part of it. You and Senator Barnes will have an opportunity to talk in depth about that, and I think you would be wise to incorporate some of his views into your testimony."

"That shouldn't be difficult," Lance said, "since the senator and I don't have any serious disagreements on policy. We'll need a considerable expansion, though, if our charter is changed."

"Yes, and you might give some thought to exactly how you want to expand. You and Kate can spend some time on that."

"Yes, sir. I will value her advice, of course."

"Thank you, Lance," Kate said, smiling. "I wouldn't have expected you to say anything else. Do you have any immediate thoughts?"

"Well," Lance said, "I think I would like to make Holly Barker's appointment as New York station chief permanent. I think she's perfect for it."

"I agree entirely," Kate said.

"I had thought of sending her to London after the trouble there, but her recommendation for the replacement there was perfectly considered, and I was glad to accept her judgment."

"I've often thought that Holly's coming to us later in life than usual, after her military and police background, gave her better judgment than we're accustomed to in recruits."

"I entirely agree," Lance said. "She has always been solid on that score, and she's a good judge of people, too. That will serve her well in New York."

"You have to understand, Lance, that if things go badly in New York, everything could change."

"I can see how that might affect things," Lance replied.

"It's better that I be here to take the blame, if things go south," Kate said. "I think that will help protect your appointment."

A butler came into the room and announced dinner.

"Of course, this is all just between us and Senator Barnes, until we're ready to move," the president said.

"I understand, sir. I would like your permission to tell Holly about it."

"That's a good idea, Will," Kate said.

"I agree," the president said, and they went in to dinner.

Lance took some deep breaths and tried to calm himself. His brain was bursting with what he wanted to do in the job.

52

The phone at Stone's bedside was ringing when they entered his bedroom. "Hello."

"It's Dino, pal. How you doing?"

"Hey, buddy, how was the Bahamas?"

"Terrific," Dino said. "Place called The Albany, on New Providence. Lap of luxury."

"You deserve it. How did Viv like the place?"

"She wants to live there."

"I'll bet she does."

"How's Holly?"

"Busier than you would believe."

"Yeah, I caught the president's speech on TV. Any leads on Jasmine?"

"Not yet, but the commissioner has really turned out the troops in the search for her. Something's got to break soon."

"I'll see what I can do about that when I get to the office tomorrow. In the meantime, I've got some news."

"Shoot."

"Viv and I are going to get legal."

"You're kidding me."

"I kid you not. She's turning in her papers tomorrow. She's got her twenty in, so she'll get her pension."

"How about you?"

"Me? Turn in my papers? You must be hallucinating."

"When's the wedding?"

"We're working on that. It'll be soon."

"Why don't the two of you come over here tomorrow night, and I'll crack a bottle of champagne and cook dinner for us."

"Deal, but it'll have to be late. We've got something to do early. Nine be okay?"

"Nine it is. See you then." Stone hung up and turned to Holly, who was just coming out of her dressing room, beautifully naked. "That was Dino. He and Viv are just back from the Bahamas, and they're going to get married."

"I don't believe it."

"Neither did I, but they're coming to dinner tomorrow night at nine, so you can grill them about it."

"I'll do that." A phone began to ring in Holly's dressing room. "I have to get that," she said. She went back and answered her cell phone.

"Good evening. It's Lance."

"Hey, Lance, what's up?"

"Quite a lot, actually."

"You're not going to get me out of bed, are you?"

"No, nothing like that. I had dinner with the president and first lady tonight. I just got in."

"I saw them when they were in New York," she said.

"They invited me over to watch him deliver his address to the nation, then dinner. Did you see it?"

"I did, and I thought it went very well."

"There's something in the offing, and I wanted you to know about it — so does Kate."

"She didn't mention anything when she was in New York."

"This really just happened today. Kate is now planning to resign before the end of Will's second term."

Holly was thunderstruck. "She certainly didn't mention that."

"The president is going to appoint me as her successor. That way he can get me confirmed before he leaves office."

"That's terrific news, Lance. How do you think it will go in Congress?"

"Senator Barnes of Georgia, the chairman of the Senate Select Committee on Intelligence, is already on board with it, and as Barnes goes, so goes the committee and the Senate."

"Then it's a done deal?"

"For all practical purposes. Barnes is also going to get the amendment to our charter through, as well."

"That's good news."

"This is going to have a big effect on your career, Holly."

"Oh?" Here it came; Lance was going to bring her back to Langley as his assistant director.

"With the change in the charter in effect, I'm going to make the New York office a permanent station, and I want you to run it."

Holly's heart leaped; she couldn't speak.

"Are you there, Holly?"

"Yes, I'm just trying to catch my breath."

"I know you wouldn't want to go back to being my assistant, and with our new domestic duties, New York is going to become our most important station. It's our only office in the country that's already fully up and running, and you've already been appointed acting station head. We'll make your appointment permanent."

"Oh, Lance, that would be just great."

"Then you accept?"

"Are you kidding? Of course I accept."

"Good, then all our ducks are in a row. There's just one thing, though."

Holly's heart was in her throat; Lance always had a hole card that nobody but he saw.

"What's that?"

"We've got to bag Jasmine. Kate can't retire while that's undone."

Holly sagged with relief; she had been expecting something self-serving from Lance. "I can understand that, and I'm on it."

"If Kate stays on until the end of Will's term, the next president will appoint her replacement, and we don't know who that president or his appointee will be. Maybe me, maybe not, but I'd feel a lot better if we could bag Jasmine and present the new president with a fait accompli. That would be much better for both you and me. And probably for the country."

"I can't argue with that," Holly said.

"And when we bag Jasmine, she has to *stay* bagged."

A little shiver went up Holly's spine; now she knew what was coming.

"That means we need to bag her while she's still in New York. It's the only place in the country where we're strong. If she's able to run and the FBI gets her somewhere else, then it will be out of our hands. The trials could go on for years."

"I see what you mean," Holly said.

"Do you? Do you understand fully what's at stake? Are you prepared to make it happen?"

"I'll do whatever I can," Holly said.

"That's not good enough. Her two brothers and Dr. Kharl are gone. Jasmine has to join them in whatever hell they're in."

Holly took a deep breath. "I'm on board with that, Lance. You can count on me."

"Good. Now get a good night's sleep, then go get her. Good night."

"Good night." They both hung up, and Holly walked back into the bedroom.

Stone saw the look on her face. "What's wrong?"

"That was Lance." She related the substance of their conversation.

"Making your appointment in New York permanent is great news."

"Yes," she said, "but I've also been appointed Jasmine's executioner."

53

Holly was in her office the following morning when Scotty buzzed her. "The director on line one," she said.

Holly picked up the phone. "Good morning, Director," she said.

"Good morning, Holly. Did Lance call you last night?"

"Yes, he did."

"I wanted to tell you the news, but Lance was eager to speak to you first."

"I'm delighted for Lance," Holly said, "but I'm going to miss you. I thought we still had a few months."

"Will and I talked about it a lot, and we finally agreed that the best way to ensure continuity at the Agency was to get the right person in the job as soon as possible, and I believe Lance is the right person. You'd have to go back a long way to find a director who came out of operations. The professionals who've had the job have been analysts, like me."

"I agree with you entirely, and I'm very happy with the idea of having my temporary appointment in New York made permanent. The time I've spent here has reminded me of how much I love this city."

"I love it, too, and I'm looking forward to sitting on Strategic Services' board when Will leaves office."

"I hope I'll see a lot of you then."

"You will. Anything new on the search for Jasmine?"

"I'm expecting a call from the commissioner momentarily — we speak nearly every morning. The FBI has been eerily quiet, for which I'm grateful."

"I think it's best not to disturb them, unless we have to. When we get a line on the al Qaeda cells in the other cities, then we'll need their help to break them up. Even if the change in our charter is made permanent, we'll need to staff up around the country, and that will take time. I'm already looking at recruiting more people and expanding the program at the Farm."

"Sounds good."

"I'll let you know. Call me if the commissioner has anything new."

"I'll do that." Both women hung up, and

a moment later Scotty buzzed that the commissioner was on the line.

"Good morning, Holly."

"Good morning, Commissioner."

"An update: Stone's idea about Middle Eastern restaurants that deliver is producing leads. We've had a dozen or more calls from people who believe they've seen something interesting on deliveries. Nothing that's checked out yet, though."

"She seems to have gone all quiet," Holly said. "Either Jasmine has moved on to another city, or she's planning something new here."

"I'm inclined to think she's still here," the commissioner said, "and I'm proceeding on that basis."

"I think that's wise. You and I can't cover five other cities. We'll have to leave that to the FBI."

"That seems to be their plan," he said. "I spoke to Deputy Director Kerry Smith in D.C. yesterday, and they're moving agents out of New York to the other cities as we speak. I'm glad to have them off my back here. I much prefer working with you."

"Thank you, Commissioner."

"I hope that, in light of your charter change, you'll stay on in New York, Holly."

"I'd like that, but it's not up to me. We'll

see what happens. I hope we can get a line on Jasmine without another bomb going off."

"We have a very large emergency response team set up in that event," the commissioner said.

"Good."

"I'll speak to you tomorrow," he said, and they both hung up.

Holly thought that if her assignment was made permanent, she'd be seeing a lot more of the commissioner, perhaps as mayor. The papers had been full of rumors that he was thinking of running. She and Lance were not the only ones who would benefit from putting Jasmine out of business.

Scotty buzzed that the people for her mid-morning staff meeting had arrived, and they filed in and took their seats at her conference table.

"All right," Holly said, "I've just spoken to the commissioner, and he tells me that they're getting calls from Middle Eastern restaurants offering leads. What have we got here?"

A young analyst raised his hand. "I have an opinion about something," he said.

"Let's hear it."

"I've been looking for factors that might allow us to predict where a new attack in the city might occur."

"I'm all ears."

"The attacks in London were against MI-6, and the two here have been against us. It seems that Jasmine isn't just interested in causing havoc — she hates intelligence services, too."

"So, you think she might try again here?" Holly asked.

"Not this building," the young man said. "And if she did, we've pretty much got that covered with our recent upgrade of security and surveillance."

"Where, then?"

"Not where," he said, "who. Excuse me, whom."

"All right, whom?"

"You, Chief."

Holly stared at him. "I suppose that makes sense, since I'm in charge."

"It's not just that," he said. "You're staying at a friend's house, I believe."

"That's correct."

"That makes you vulnerable."

"We've got security posted at the house."

"Security can't stop a truck full of explosives from driving past the house."

Holly leaned back in her chair. "So what's your recommendation?"

"I think you should move back into our

building," he said, "and I don't think you should leave the building again until Jasmine has been apprehended or killed."

"We could increase security around the house," his supervisor said.

"No, he's right," Holly said.

"I don't mean to offend," the young man said.

"You haven't offended me by being right," Holly replied. "I'll move back in here today."

"I think we'd all feel better," he said.

Then Holly remembered that she and Stone had Dino and Viv coming for dinner that night, to celebrate their engagement. "I'll move back in tonight," she said. "I'll need to go and pick up my things first."

When the meeting was over she called Stone and explained that she had to move.

"I'm sorry to hear it," he said.

"I'm sorry, too, but my own staff has pointed out to me that I'm a probable target, and they're right. I'll leave our security in place at your house, though."

"If you're gone, then what's the problem here?"

"Jasmine may not know I'm gone."

"She may not know you were here in the first place."

"I can't count on that. What time are Dino

339

and Viv coming tonight?"

"Not until nine — they both had something to do earlier."

"Then I'll be home by nine."

"See you then."

Holly hung up, not looking forward to moving into this cold, hard building.

54

Dino, wearing his uniform, stood at attention and watched the commissioner pin the medal on Viv's tunic, the decoration she had won by shooting a fugitive and saving his life. Everyone applauded, then the senior uniformed officer present dismissed the group, who adjourned to a conference room for champagne.

The commissioner approached Dino. "We're proud of her," he said, "and I'm sorry she retired today. What's she going to do with herself?"

"It'll be announced in a few days," Dino said, "so keep this under your hat. She's joining Strategic Services as an investigative supervisor."

"It occurs to me that she might be available for another role, as well," the commissioner said.

Dino grinned. "I can't comment on that at the moment, but maybe soon."

"What are your plans, Dino?"

"Oh, more of the same, sir."

"I wish you'd take the captain's exam. I could use you at headquarters, but you can't be a lieutenant among so many captains."

"Commissioner, the minute I pass the captain's exam, I'm not a cop anymore, I'm an administrator."

The commissioner shrugged. "I can't argue with that, but I think you could be very useful to me in this office."

"I like solving crimes," Dino said. "And I like kicking detectives' asses until they get it right."

"Tell you what," the commissioner said, "sit the exam next week and pass, and I'll sit on the result until you say it's okay."

"Why would you want me to do that?" Dino asked.

"I have my reasons," the commissioner replied, "and I promise you, you'll like them when you know what they are."

Dino cocked his head and examined the commissioner's face for clues to what he was talking about, but all he got for his trouble was a hint of a smirk.

"I can still stay in my job if I do that?"

"I won't yank you out of the one-nine unless it's what you want, I promise you that."

"All right, Commissioner, I'll take the

exam, but I hope I don't disappoint you by flunking."

The commissioner took a pad from his coat pocket, jotted down a name and number, ripped it out and handed it to Dino. "Call this man tomorrow morning and report to him on Monday morning. He'll cram enough in your skull to see that you don't flunk."

Dino looked at the name, and he knew the man: a retired captain who had been in charge of administering examinations for the last years of his career. "Yes, sir," he said.

Later, as he and Viv were driven away from police headquarters in Dino's car, he took off his hat and loosened his tie. "I'm going to have to lose a few pounds before I feel comfortable in this uniform," he said.

"You look good in it now," Viv said, patting his knee.

"We'll drop you at your place to change, then I'll pick you up later."

"I'll get a cab to Stone's house. I'll be just a little later than you. It takes girls longer."

"It's just the four of us," Dino said.

"Nevertheless."

Dino sighed. "Okay, okay, I'll go on ahead of you."

Half an hour later, Dino's driver, a rookie detective, pulled into a vacant spot across the street from Stone's house. "Get yourself some dinner," Dino said to the young man. "I'm going to be here for a while."

"Yessir," the detective replied. He got out of the car, opened the door for Dino, then reached into the front seat and came up with two orange traffic cones. As Dino crossed the street, the detective placed them so as to save his parking spot, then he got back into the car and drove away.

Dino rapped on the darkened window of the black SUV parked in front of Stone's house, and the window slid down. He held up his badge. "Lieutenant Bacchetti," he said. "Detective DeCarlo will be along in a few minutes."

"Go right in, Lieutenant," the young security man said.

Dino trotted up the front steps and rang the bell.

"Yes?"

"It's Dino."

"I'm in the study. I'll buy you a drink."

The door lock clicked open, and Dino let himself into the house.

■ ■ ■ ■

Stone was already pouring the drinks as Dino walked into the study. "Hey, there," Stone said. "Did Viv get decorated?"

Dino accepted the drink and settled into a chair. "Yep, and the commissioner got all funny with me."

"How so?"

"He insisted I take the captain's exam, but promised not to make me take the rank. What do you make of that?"

"I think the commissioner never does anything without a good reason, and you should take his advice."

"I'll have to spend some time with a retired captain, cramming for it."

"You were always good at the exams," Stone said. "You'll ace it first time."

"It makes me nervous," Dino said.

"You're afraid he'll give you a precinct and cuff you to a desk?"

"That or make a politician out of me."

"The man knows you well, Dino, and he's always liked you. He's not going to fuck you."

"If you say so."

Stone set his drink on the coffee table, went to a cabinet, and opened it, revealing a safe. He punched in the combination, fished out a small velvet box, then locked the safe again. "I have a present for you," he said, tossing it to Dino.

Dino opened the box, and found a substantial diamond ring. He gave a low whistle. "Nice rock. You proposing to me?"

"It's the ring I bought Arrington all those years ago, when I was about to propose to her. Then, of course, Vance Calder shot me out of the saddle, and life changed. You're going to need a ring, and I know you well enough to know that you hate that kind of shopping. I want you to have this to give to Viv."

"Well, that would stun her," Dino said.

"She'll enjoy the experience," Stone said. "Women like diamonds, and I have no further use for that one."

Dino seemed to have trouble speaking. "Thanks, pal," he finally managed to say.

55

Stone, Dino, and Viv were having a glass of wine in the kitchen while Stone stirred his risotto, adding stock every minute or so. Holly came in and dropped her bag on the floor with a loud thud.

"I need a real drink," she said. "Not wine, booze."

"Right over there," Stone said, nodding toward the kitchen bar. "I can't put down my spoon right now."

"What's in the bag?" Dino asked. "A mortar?"

"Just my sidearm and three loaded magazines," Holly said. "It adds up."

"Three magazines? You expecting trouble?"

"I'm afraid so," Holly replied, splashing bourbon into a glass filled with ice. "One of my people convinced me I might be next on Jasmine's list of favorite people."

"Why are we having dinner with her,

Stone?" Dino asked. "Aren't we in danger?"

"I'll chance it," Stone said. "Anyway, she lives here, we can't throw her out."

"Not for long," Holly said, gulping down some bourbon. "I'm moving into our New York station after dinner. You'll all be safe then."

"I'm glad you're here," Dino said. "I want witnesses, and Stone isn't enough."

"Witnesses?" Viv asked.

Dino set the velvet box on the table and opened it. "Will you marry me?"

Viv stared at the ring. "I notice that you put the ring on the table before you asked. Are you trying to buy me?"

"Whatever works," Dino said. "I can't live without you, and Stone and Holly are witnesses that I said that, because we both know I might try to weasel out of it later."

Viv removed the ring from the box and slipped it on. "It fits," she said.

"Of course it fits," Dino replied. "It's yours. Now answer me, please."

"I forgot the question."

"Love, marriage, death do us part?"

"Yeah, okay, that works for me."

Dino put a hand on her face and kissed her. "Thank God we got that out of the way," he said. "Now we can eat."

"Five minutes," Stone said, stirring in a

fistful of grated Parmigiano-Reggiano, then prying open a carton of crème fraîche and spooning half of it into the pan. He added more of the cheese, then raked in a plate of shrimp and a bowl of asparagus tips.

"That looks good," Holly said, polishing off her bourbon, then pouring herself a glass of wine.

"I've had it before," Dino said. "You won't die from eating it."

"High praise, Dino," Stone said, putting a trivet on the table and setting the pan on it. He slid into the banquette beside Holly and raised his wineglass. "Dino and Viv," he said. "May they not kill each other the first year."

They all drank.

Across town Habib sat at the kitchen table with a block of C4 explosive, a detonator, some wire, and a throwaway cell phone. He used a soldering iron to make the connections, then plugged one end of the wire into the cell phone and the end with the detonator into the soft C4.

"There you are," he said, "one bomb."

"You're sure this will set off the rest?"

"My bombs go off when they're told to," Habib said. "The other forty-nine kilos are already in the van. All I have to do is place this block with the others, then you can have the honor of detonating." He pushed another cell phone across the table. "It's already programmed. All you have to do is press one, and it will autodial the correct number. The detonator will fire on the first ring: then *poof*! No more Ms. Barker or Mr. Barrington."

"Do we know they're there now?"

"We assume Barrington is there. Two other people, a man and a woman, arrived earlier and checked in with the guards in the SUV. Holly Barker arrived twenty minutes ago. I told our observer to get out of there."

"Then we're all set?"

"We are. The van and the Toyota you wanted for our trip are parked outside, and our luggage is in the trunk. You blow it after leaving Barrington's street — on Forty-second Street, headed for the tunnel. Fifteen minutes after that we'll be in New Jersey, headed west."

"Why can't we blow it from New Jersey? I'd feel safer."

"We can't leave the van there untended any longer than absolutely necessary. Some traffic cop might take exception and screw things up. Don't worry, Forty-second Street is plenty far away, and it won't take long to get there. Once we turn onto Second Avenue the traffic signals are programmed to change as we drive downtown. We have only two turns to make, so it will go smoothly."

"All right," Jasmine said. "Let's do it."

56

They were on their second helpings of risotto and their second bottle of Far Niente Chardonnay. Stone looked at his friends and felt good. He had never seen Dino happier.

"Okay," Stone said, "when's the wedding?"

"Don't rush me," Dino said.

"Who's rushing you?" Stone asked.

"Yeah, who's rushing you?" Viv echoed. "How about a week from tomorrow in the police chapel?"

"That sounds wonderful," Holly chipped in.

"What's the hurry?" Dino asked. "I haven't even gotten used to being engaged yet."

"You're not supposed to get used to it," Holly said. "That way lies delay after delay."

"She has a point, Dino," Stone said, patting him on the shoulder in a fatherly manner.

"But where are we going to live?" Dino asked plaintively.

"Last time I checked," Viv said, "and that was this morning, you have an apartment, I have an apartment. Take your pick."

"Well, you know I'm not going to pick yours," Dino said.

"Good, that leaves yours."

"It's not big enough — it's a bachelor apartment, for God's sake."

"It's plenty big," Viv said.

"There's not enough closet space for your underwear, let alone everything else."

"I don't intend to wear much underwear for a while," Viv said. "That will leave room for my other stuff."

"You could get rid of some of those old suits that are moldering away in your closets," Stone said. "You've had some of them since high school."

"Those are perfectly good clothes that I'll wear again," Dino protested.

"Not as long as the trousers won't button," Stone pointed out.

"There's another alternative," Viv said. "We could sell both our apartments and buy a bigger one."

Dino seemed struck dumb.

"Aha, you've got him," Holly said, giggling.

"I'm thinking it over," Dino said.

The others stared at him, determined to wait him out. Dino squirmed.

Jasmine turned into the street and spotted the black SUV immediately. She took the 9mm silenced pistol from her handbag and shoved it between her legs. Habib would shortly be behind her.

She coasted to a stop inches from the SUV's blackened windows, rolled her own window down, and yelled, "Excuse me!" Nothing happened. It must be very thick, armored glass, she thought. She reached out the window and rapped very hard on it with her ring. A moment later, the window slid halfway down.

"Yes?" a wary voice asked.

"Excuse me, could you direct me —" Then she took the silenced 9mm from between her legs and shot them both in the head.

Junior Detective Sean Leary turned back into the block, a sandwich on the seat beside him, and saw twin flashes emanating from between the black CIA SUV and a white car pulled up close to it, but heard nothing. "Gunshots fired," he said aloud to himself. "Silencer." He accelerated and rammed the white car from behind, shoving it down the street. He saw its brake lights come on, and a woman was suddenly running toward him, a gun in her hand. He was digging at his waist for his own weapon as she reached his car, holding out the silenced pistol.

Then, as she fired, his own car was rammed from behind, shoving him forward into the Toyota for a second time. Leary opened his door and rolled into the street, in a prone firing position. He felt something strike him hard in the back, and he put his head down and began firing wildly in her general direction.

"Well, Dino?" Stone asked.

Dino's mouth was working, but nothing was coming out.

Then they heard an unmistakable sound: a gunshot, followed by five more.

"Thirty-eight," Viv said.

One second after the final gunshot, Stone's security system went off, and loudly.

"They're shooting at the house," Stone said as they all scrambled out of the banquette.

Stone ran through the lower level of the house from the kitchen, through his exercise room to his office, then down the hall toward the front door. He ducked into

Joan's office and retrieved her .45 from her desk drawer, and as he did, Dino blew past him in the hallway, weapon in hand, and out the office door into the street. Stone followed on his heels, just ahead of Viv and Holly, who were also armed.

Habib grabbed Jasmine's arm. "We've got to go!" he yelled. He half dragged her to the car and shoved her into the passenger side, then ran around the car. As he opened the driver's door he saw people spilling out of the house behind him, and they were armed. The engine was still running, and he floored the car. He was just feeling lucky that it was still running when he had to slam on brakes to stop from running into a truck stopped in front of him. He leaned on the horn.

"White car, down the block!" Holly yelled, then ran in that direction, followed closely by Viv.

But Dino wasn't looking at the car, he was looking through a window of the van with the damaged front end, stopped in the middle of the street. He tried to open both doors: locked. He banged on the glass with the butt of his pistol, to no avail. He looked to his left and saw Leary, lying on his belly, with blood on his back, then he turned toward Stone, who was standing beside him.

"Get something to break this glass!" he yelled.

"Who do you think is in there?" Stone yelled back.

"Nobody. It's gotta be a bomb!"

Stone turned and ran up the front steps and into the house.

Dino went to Leary. "Kid, talk to me!"

"I'm okay, I think," Leary said, struggling to a knee.

"Stay right there!" Dino jumped through the open car door, one knee on the driver's seat, and reached across to open the glove compartment. He began grabbing stuff and throwing it onto the floor, until he found what he was looking for.

Habib gave up blowing the horn, stepped out of the car with one foot and aimed his gun at the truck driver, who was coming toward him. "Get that truck out of here, or I'll kill you," Habib yelled, firing a shot into a nearby car for emphasis. The man ran for his truck, and it began to roll toward Second Avenue.

Holly ran toward the white car and waved for Viv to take the passenger side, but when they were nearly there, the car shot forward, mounted the curb and began bulldozing its way toward Second Avenue.

Dino got back to the van just after Stone broke the rear window with a golf club. "Get outta the way!" he yelled at Stone, then he reached inside for the door lock. The seats had been removed from the rear of the van, and there was a large object on the floor, hidden by a raincoat thrown over it. He snatched away the coat and found a neat cube of gray bricks with a cell phone taped to the stack. "Oh, shit," he said. "Get back!"

Stone looked inside and reached for the cell phone, but Dino shoved him out of the way and onto his ass in the street. "It's gonna be booby-trapped!" he yelled. He held up the black object in his hand and pressed a button. A green light came on, and Dino set it on top of the pile of explosives. "Stay away from it!" he yelled at Stone, who was getting to his feet.

Dino ran back to Leary and dug the hand-held radio out of the man's inside coat pocket. "Just relax, Leary," he said. "Help is on the way." Dino took a deep breath and hoped for the best. He pressed the button on the side of the radio and said, "Mayday! Mayday! Mayday! This is Lieutenant Dino Bacchetti, code red, code red!" He gave the address. "I've got a very large bomb in a van and an officer down. I need ambulances and the bomb squad. Code red on Second

Avenue in the Forties!"

Stone ran up to him. "We've got to get out of here, Dino!" he said.

"It's too late to run," Dino replied.

Habib was knocking down garbage cans and scattering pedestrians.

"I'm going to blow it!" Jasmine yelled.

"Not yet! You'll kill us, too!" He made it to Second Avenue and turned right.

Holly and Viv were running as hard as they could toward the car when it turned onto Second Avenue and started to move faster. Then, suddenly, the car stopped, as did all the traffic on Second Avenue. She looked down the street and saw red traffic lights as far as the eye could see. "We've got to kill both those people now!" she yelled at Viv. They both stopped running. "I'll take the driver!" Holly raised her weapon and fired two shots. The rear window of the Toyota turned white, and she started running toward the driver's door, her weapon held ready in front of her.

Viv ran for the passenger door, and when she was ten yards away, it opened and a woman rolled out of the car and into the street, ending up on one knee, her hands out, holding a silenced pistol. Viv heard a little whir, and her hair blew back on her left side. She didn't bother aiming, just started firing, aiming at the center of the woman. She knew she had hit her at least once, but the woman didn't fall. Instead, with her free hand, she flipped open a cell phone and with a thumb, pressed a button.

"NOOO!" Viv yelled, then emptied her magazine into the crouching figure. Viv hit the street and waited for the explosion.

57

Nothing happened. Viv lifted her head and looked at the woman she had just shot several times. She was smiling. Viv reached over, grabbed the silencer, and pulled the weapon from her grasp.

Jasmine was trying to say something. Viv leaned closer and listened. "They will all die," Jasmine whispered.

Viv picked up the cell phone lying near her hand and looked at it. The word "CALLING" was on the screen, then it changed to "CALL FAILED." She held the phone in front of Jasmine's face. "Not today, sweetheart," she said. "Just you."

Jasmine frowned, then her face relaxed and her pupils dilated.

"The driver is dead," Holly said from behind her.

Viv placed two fingers on the left side of Jasmine's throat and felt for a pulse. "So is this one," she said.

Holly was on the phone.

Stone stared at Dino. "What is that thing with the green light?" he asked.

"A couple of weeks ago, Viv and I went to the theater, and there were cell phones ringing all around us, all through the first act. I saw that thing in a catalogue and ordered it. It creates a dead zone big enough to fill a room."

"It must work, then," Stone said. Then, as he watched, the green light went out.

Dino picked up the little box, opened the battery compartment, and fiddled with the single AA battery. The light came back on.

The sound of sirens and whoopers filled the air, and suddenly the street was full of flashing lights and men in body armor. Dino held his badge high, so they could see it. "On the job, guys!" he yelled. "Get me a bomb guy over here."

A moment later, a man in really big armor and a helmet with a plastic shield over his face appeared. "What have we got here?"

"Very large bomb," Dino said, pointing into the van.

"Holy shit!" the man said.

"That little box with the green light made a dead zone in the car, but you'd better get that thing disconnected before it blows. It's probably booby-trapped."

"Get the hell out of here, both of you," the man said, and Stone and Dino retreated into the house and sat down in Joan's office. "Where are the girls?" Stone asked.

"They took off after a white car," Dino said, producing his cell phone and pressing a speed dial button. He turned on the speaker. The call failed.

"It's your black box," Stone said.

Dino kept trying.

"Yeah?" Viv said.

"It's Dino. Where are you and Holly?"

"On Second Avenue. We shot two people in a white Toyota, a man and a woman. I think the woman is Jasmine."

"God, I hope you're right," Dino said.

"She made a call on a cell phone before I could stop her," Viv said, "but the call failed."

"Turn off that cell phone," Dino said. "It's real important."

"Holly's checking out the trunk of the Toyota," Viv said. "Hang on, we've got a laptop!"

"There will be cops all over you in a minute," Dino said. "I think Holly gets custody of the laptop."

"She's already called somebody," Viv said.

"Why are all the lights on Second Avenue red?"

"I called in a code red," Dino said.

"Good call, Dino. If they'd had a green light, they'd be gone."

"I'll tell the commissioner you said so."

"We'll come back to Stone's house as soon as the scene is squared away," Viv said.

"Hurry," Dino replied, and hung up.

"Dino," Stone said, "how much explosive matter was in that van? What's your guess?"

"I dunno — forty, fifty kilos, maybe."

Stone heaved a deep sigh. "I'm going to get one of those black boxes," he said. "Could you use a drink?"

"Is the Pope a mackerel snapper?"

Holly and Viv went through four suitcases in the trunk. "I got an iPhone from the purse on the car seat, but this is just clothes and stuff," Holly said.

"Except for that laptop," Viv replied. She looked up and saw a dozen uniforms running up Second Avenue toward them. "You get out of here with the computer and the iPhone," Viv said. "I'll deal with the uniforms."

"Do you still have a badge?"

Viv produced a small shield. "Just my retirement shield, but it'll work. She held it up and shouted, "On the job, fellas!" as they surrounded the car.

Holly held up her own ID. "CIA!"

Everybody relaxed.

58

Holly ran the dozen blocks to the Agency building, pacing herself, using her cell phone to call ahead. "I'm inbound on foot," she said to the duty officer. "I've got a hot Mac Air and an iPhone, and we need to lift everything from it, even if it's coded."

"We've got an NSA lady who's in town to retrain our tech guys for new software," the officer said.

"Find her and get her to the building right now," Holly said. "I'll be there in six minutes." She broke the connection and pressed her speed dial button for the police commissioner.

"Holly? Where the hell are you? We got a code red from Dino Bacchetti, and I've flooded Turtle Bay and Second Avenue with personnel."

"Frank, Jasmine is dead, and I have her laptop and cell phone. I'm headed to my office now, and we've got an NSA tech in town who can help us with it."

"I'll be there just as soon as we've cleared the Turtle Bay scene," the commissioner said.

"See you then." Holly hung up and called Stone.

"Hey, where are you?"

"On the way to my office with Jasmine's laptop and phone."

"Why are you panting?"

"Because I'm running. Don't expect me back there tonight."

"I understand." He told her about Dino's black box.

"Brilliant! I'm going to order dozens! Gotta go." She hung up and ran up to the door of her building. The security guard recognized her and buzzed her in. "Where's the duty officer?" she asked the man.

"In the ops room, two floors down," he replied.

She pressed the elevator button, then rode down.

An hour and a half later, the NSA tech called Holly in her office. "Got it all," she said. "The files were encoded, but it was no match for our computer."

"E-mail me the pages now," Holly said. She hung up and turned to the commissioner, who was sitting on her sofa, drinking coffee. "We're into her computer," she said. "They're sending me what they found."

"Good news!"

"We're due for some," Holly said. She opened her mail program and printed out two copies of the files, then handed the commissioner a stack of papers.

He scanned the pages quickly. "I don't believe our luck," he said. "There's contact information for each of the other four cells in the other cities."

"We're going to need the FBI for this," Holly said. "They're the only ones who have people on the ground in these cities."

"You want to call them, or should I?"

"I think that should be done director to director," Holly said, then called the White House switchboard and asked for Kate Lee.

"Holly? What's going on in New York with Jasmine's computer?"

"We've broken into her laptop. We have locations for the four al Qaeda cells in the other cities, and I think you should get them to the FBI."

"I'll call the director," Kate said.

"I'll e-mail you both the pages. Please tell him it's important they all be hit at the same time."

"I'll do that and call you back." She hung up.

"Kate's on it," she said to the commissioner. She e-mailed the files from the laptop and the phone to both directors.

"I've already told my deputy for public affairs to keep a lid on this until he gets my order."

"Then all we can do for now is wait," Holly said. "By the way, it was Viv DeCarlo who put Jasmine down. Check the ballistics. You should be proud of her."

"I've always been proud of her," the commissioner said, "and I hate to lose her. She retired today."

"I know, we had dinner together earlier this evening."

"I just thought of something," the commissioner said.

"What?"

"Never mind. Let me check it out before I break it to you." He got out his phone and walked down to the other end of the room.

Holly looked at her watch: it was two A.M. Her phone rang. "Holly Barker."

"It's Kate. The director says he can hit all four cells simultaneously in three hours. He's already given the orders."

"At five a.m., then," Holly said.

"Take a nap," Kate said. "I'll call you

when I hear something."

Holly walked over to her sofa and stretched out. The commissioner was still on his phone. She took a deep breath, let it out, and dozed off.

59

Stone was having his breakfast in bed while watching *Morning Joe.* "We've just heard that the president will be making an important announcement shortly," Scarborough said, "and we're switching to the *Today* show for that."

The White House press secretary appeared on-screen. "Ladies and gentlemen, the president of the United States." The White House press corps leaped to their feet as the president took the stage.

"Good morning," Will Lee said. "Last night in New York City a failed bombing attack resulted in the deaths of two CIA security officers and two al Qaeda terrorists. Jasmine Shazaz, who was wanted in both New York and London for recent bombing attacks, and her principal henchman died in a gunfight with a CIA officer and a retired NYPD detective, both of whom emerged unhurt. This event was made possible by an NYPD rapid response effort that had been put into effect only in the past few weeks, along with intelligence from the British counterintelligence service, MI-6. Following the deaths of the two al Qaeda operatives, a laptop computer and a cell phone found in their vehicle were unencrypted by the NSA, and as a result, FBI SWAT teams, in conjunction with police officers from the relevant jurisdictions, conducted raids in four other cities — Boston, Chicago, Los Angeles, and Atlanta — that resulted in the deaths or capture of nineteen al Qaeda terrorists and the wounding of two FBI agents, both of whom were treated in local hospitals and are now recovering at home.

"This remarkable, coordinated effort on the part of two federal agencies, a foreign intelligence service, and five local police departments has made the most emphatic statement since the killing of Osama bin Laden that the United States and her ally, Great Britain, will meet and destroy every effort made to harm our people through terrorism. I congratulate all the officers involved and their commanders on a superb effort. Because of security restraints, I will not be responding to questions on this occasion, but more information will be released by the White House as it becomes confirmed and available. Thank you."

The president turned and walked from the stage as the press began shouting questions at the press secretary.

Stone switched to three other stations and found the same thing on each of them. After he had showered, shaved, and dressed, the story was still running on all channels. As he was about to go downstairs, Holly arrived, exhausted but elated.

Stone embraced her. "Congratulations on a great night."

"Did you see the president on television?" she asked.

"Yes, and he was perfect."

"Where are Dino and Viv?"

"At home asleep, I hope."

"Viv was wonderful," Holly said. "It was she who shot Jasmine before the woman could shoot me."

"That's two villains she's taken out this year," Stone said.

"That's right — she got her medal for taking out Shelley Bach, didn't she?"

"And saving Dino's ass."

"And Dino saved all our asses with his little black box."

"You're absolutely right. I think by way of thanks we should throw his and Viv's wedding reception here."

"It's the least we can do."

"You're exhausted. Get some sleep. There's no more you can do today. I'll tell Joan to cut the phones off up here."

Holly nodded. "First a soak in the tub, then sleep."

Stone went and ran her bath while she undressed.

"Don't drown," he said, as she sank into the hot water.

60

The living room and dining room of Stone's house were filled with a hundred or so guests, most of them cops, celebrating Dino and Viv's wedding, which a judge had legalized in the garden an hour before.

A jazz trio was filling the rooms with music, and as they finished a number, the police commissioner stepped forward, took the microphone, and called for everyone's attention.

"I have a few words — very few words to say — about the honorees this evening. A couple of weeks ago I was pleased to award the Police Combat Cross to Viv DeCarlo on the occasion of her retirement from the NYPD. Now I have the doubly great honor of awarding our highest decoration to Vivian DeCarlo Bacchetti and her new husband, Lieutenant Dino Bacchetti. The Medal of Honor is awarded for acts of gallantry and valor performed with knowledge of the risk involved, above and beyond the call of duty, and the actions of both Viv and Dino rose to that level on the night in question. Together, they saved many, many lives and rid our city of a vile terrorist who had already done us great harm." The commissioner pinned the medals on the newlyweds, to the cheering and applause of all present.

The music started again, and the crowd rushed forward to congratulate the couple, then they resumed dancing.

Stone and Holly were standing with Dino and Viv when the commissioner approached, swept them into Stone's study, and closed the door behind them. "There's more," the commissioner said. "First of all, tomorrow Detective Sean Leary will be awarded the Police Combat Cross for his actions on that night."

"He deserves it," Dino said.

"Also," the commissioner said, removing an envelope from his inside pocket and handing it to Viv, "the FBI has asked me to pass along something to you. The director regrets that he was unable to join us this evening."

Viv took the envelope. "Thank you, Commissioner." She peeked inside it and gasped. "What is this?"

"It's the reward the FBI put up for taking

Jasmine out of action."

Viv turned to Dino. "We're going to start looking for a bigger apartment tomorrow."

"And one other thing," the commissioner said. "Word has reached me that Dino passed the captain's exam — and at the top of the list."

Stone shook Dino's hand and clapped him on the back.

"And there's still more," the commissioner said. "A few weeks ago, Robert Morgan told me of his intention to retire as chief of detectives, and I am promoting Dino to that office, effective the day after his return from his honeymoon."

Dino's face registered shock.

"Don't worry, Dino, you'll still be a cop," the commissioner said. "I will appoint a deputy chief of detectives for administration, who will deal with the paper. I'm perfectly aware that I'm jumping you over the heads of a dozen captains who've had more time in rank, but that's my prerogative."

"In that case, Commissioner, just to annoy all those captains, I accept," Dino said.

"I expect this news will encourage a few of them to retire, making possible a number of promotions. And there's just one more thing," the commissioner said, "then you can all go and get even drunker."

Everybody laughed.

"Tomorrow, I'm going to announce my candidacy for mayor of the City of New York, and I want you to know, Dino, that should I be elected — and I expect to be — I will not forget you."

All present applauded and shook the commissioner's hand.

"And," the commissioner finally said, "I want to congratulate Holly on her appointment as permanent chief of the New York station of the CIA."

"I think," Holly said, "that since this may be the last time I can get really drunk, we should take the chief's advice and go do it!"

"Viv," Dino said, "how much was the reward?"

Viv clasped the envelope to her bosom. "Don't ask."

Later, Stone and Holly lay in each other's arms, finally relaxed and exhausted.

"At last, with Jasmine out of the picture, we can feel safe again," Stone said.

Holly sighed. "For the moment," she replied.

ABOUT THE AUTHOR

Stuart Woods is the author of more than fifty novels, including the *New York Times'* bestselling Stone Barrington and Holly Barker series. He is a native of Georgia and began his writing career in the advertising industry. *Chiefs,* his debut in 1981, won the Edgar Award. An avid sailor and pilot, Woods lives in New York City, Florida, and Maine.